BONES

YOLANDA OLSON

BLURB

Loss is not something I'm accustomed to.
However, it's what I'm faced with now because I can't remember.
I've tried so hard to find what I'm looking for, and while I've done my best, it still eludes me.
The memory comes and goes in glimpses of a faded past and possible future, yet I can't grasp it.
Not yet.
Stay close and don't look back.
This is going to be a hard road, but we'll get through this together.

We have to.

You're the only hope I have left.

*Happy Birthday Big Sis.
Here's one just for you.*

PROLOGUE

I was always fascinated by skulls. The way they look when the skin and muscle are peeled away; the solid, smooth feel of them when they're cleaned properly makes my body ache. I wouldn't say that I'm sexually aroused by the actual skulls, it's more the detachment from the human body, the taking off the multitude of layers that makes my cock hard. I don't have many yet, but I'm getting there. Slow and steady wins the race, and all that jazz.

I'm not a serial killer.

No matter how much everyone

wants to believe it, no matter how many lies are printed about me, no matter what story you choose to believe. Serial killers have a compulsion they can't control, and I am *very* controlled. No, I like to think that I'm just a man with a different train of thought that enjoys the macabre things in life. I like seeing how things tick, and I am absolutely elated when I get to take them apart.

As I set the skull into the cabinet that sits in my living room, I step back and smile. I have four so far, mostly women, but this is my first male skull, and it's a bit larger. *That won't do.* I retrace my steps and rearrange them, leaving the larger on a shelf by itself and setting the other three in equal separate spaces beneath it. It looks like the beginnings of a small pyramid; my own personal wonder of the world, and I can't help but feel proud of myself.

I never started with animals; another thing to distinguish me from the serial killer cliché. My home is impeccable, and there are no traces of death to be found except for what's inside the now closed glass doors of this cabinet. I like to bring people here and show them my art, letting them believe that these are props that I've found online instead of beautiful moments of distraction that have kept me company for the past few years.

I only ever needed what I've come to call a distraction four times now. The times I would act upon the urge was never the same allotment as the last. It was just when I felt it was needed. Pushing my pecan-brown, medium length hair away from where it's fallen into my eyes, I linger for just a moment longer before I walk into the kitchen and turn my coffee machine on.

Although I know it's not good for me in the long run, it's how I start my day. I can't find it in myself to put energy drinks into my body, so I compromise and allow myself one cup of coffee a day. The sound of the steady drip as it pours from the small spout of the machine gives me a moment to close my eyes and think. It had been months since I had collected that skull, but I didn't have the urge to clean it until just the night before. When I went to bed, I set it on the side-table and stared at it, a secret smile on my face, until my body relaxed enough allowing me to sleep.

That was something I wasn't every good at—sleeping. It wasn't what I did that would keep me awake at night, but rather it was what I *couldn't* do. I sometimes wished it would be easier for myself and everyone around me if I stayed inside of my home. I've even had thoughts of laying brick against the windows and the doorways to prevent me from getting out or from anyone else ever getting in.

But there would be time for that later. For now, I had to fill my cabinet, and when that was done, I would spare anyone else the same fate of the imbeciles that had been tragically trusting enough to come home with me. Some I had spared for the most part, but those four—I needed them to stave off the hunger inside of me. I was creating a beautiful sonata of the macabre for the safety of countless others, and when my cabinet was full, I would stop.

It would be easy to stop, I imagined as the drip of coffee sputtered and died. I never put cream or sugar in it, I didn't want to add to the shit I was already putting into my body. I opened my eyes, grabbed the dark green mug, and put the bitter brew to my lips, sipping slowly as I walked back into the living room and sat down on my opulent leather couch staring back at the grinning skulls.

Usually the urge doesn't hit me once I've cleaned one of my newer pieces, but as I've mentioned, this one isn't new. It's a few months old, and it's finally being displayed where it belongs. It's not my masterpiece though; that still walks in the daylight, or maybe in the moonlight depending on when I manage to run into her. So far, I've learned her name, her age, and through idiotic small talk each time we've chatted briefly, the things she happens to like.

She belongs in my cabinet; part of her does. On the top shelf, perhaps a majestic crown of sorts to always remind me that I was able to achieve the acquisition of my most prized piece for my display.

I'll look for her today. Maybe I'll find her, maybe I won't. Maybe I'll spend the day and night wandering the city aimlessly looking for someone else to place in my cabinet in lieu of her head, but there are things that I know are true. Things that anyone who deems to whisper my story needs to understand and believe.

I can stop anytime I want to.

I am *not* a serial killer.

CHAPTER ONE

I fell asleep on my couch. I didn't mean to, but I always found such a relaxing comfort in looking into the faces of death that I had helped create. I wake up to a wet sweat pant leg from where I had spilled the coffee on myself, and I sigh loudly. I'm not a messy man, and this annoys me that I had done something so *normal*.

I get to my feet and walk into the kitchen, crouching down in front of the small wooden doors in front of the sink, and pull out a stain cleaner that I use frequently. I reason that if it works on blood, it will work on coffee. And if it doesn't, I would just rip up the carpet in a rage that would sometimes descend over me, and I would get rid of it.

The rage has nothing to do with control. I *am* controlled; it is just something that happens every now and again to remind me that I am human. Maybe rage isn't the best way to describe it. Maybe severe frustration would be a better term.

I quickly walk back into the living room and drop onto my knees just close enough to the stain that I am able to spray it and let the foam set before I scrub it away. I wait almost in frantic impatience as the stain starts to turn white, the foam starting to coat it, and hovering above the spot with an old rag ready and dying to remove any trace of my unconscious misstep.

I'm *not* a messy man. The longer I hover, the more seconds that tick by, the more I want to rip my hair out. Why does it seem like it is taking so long for the foam to rise? When will it finally give me the signal to scrub away the spot of mess that is taunting me below it? It is almost as if it is laughing at me, telling me that there would be no way I will ever be able to get rid of it.

Fucking finally!

I immediately drop the rag into the raised foam and began to scrub furiously. I don't want the stain to think it won, I don't want it to believe that it could sit there, in *my* home, and mock me each time I come to look at my cabinet. This is where I come to relax and goddamn it, this fucking thing will be gone one way or the other. I refuse to share my home with it.

I'm not crazy.

I understand that this may seem like I am, but I just like to keep a tidy home. I spend a solid minute moving the rag back and forth, quickly, furiously, as deeply into the carpet as I can—beads of sweat starting to form on the side of my face until I dare to lift it and see who has won.

A victorious, smug smile spreads quickly over my face as I get to my feet. I reach down and scoop the stain remover off of the carpet and walk back into the kitchen, placing it back into its dark little home and tossing the rag into the sink. I won't be able to clean it right away, but I will open the faucet and let a generous amount of scalding hot water pour over it until it will be safe for me to touch again.

The stain cleaner is a special mixture of my own—the secret to die safely when I did. Not that it would come to pass anytime soon, but I just like the idea of having secrets. It helps me stand out when I need to, and it keeps me safe when I felt like the world is crashing down around me.

Secrets aren't always a good thing, especially not my secrets, but as I've said, it's for the sanity of myself that I keep them and the safety of others that they don't pass my lips.

Not always.

I won't tell anyone my secrets until I find her again. I'll tell her everything; a confession of sorts, get them all out of me, and then when she finally understands what goes on in my head, she'll accept her fate.

Not that I would.

But then again, I've always been something of a fighter. Not necessarily a strong man, though I do like to keep my body in shape. I believe the saying that your body is a temple, and I enjoy having a finely built structure of my very own.

I'm not vain.

Vanity is a vapid trait, and I'll have no part of it. However, I've come to find that most women, and some men, like a particular body frame, and I like to attract those people. The ones that I know will be easiest to seduce usually are used and sent on their way, but the four that I already have made love to in my mind with simple conversation.

That's how I knew I had to keep them.

I like having conversations about almost anything. Someone that can hold my attention long enough to indulge my mindless chatter is definitely someone worth keeping. I've never let any of them go except for her.

She's seduced my thoughts more than once, and I like the game of cat and mouse that we play each time we come across each other. She always leaves me in a stunned euphoria, though I never really retain much of what she says. I wasn't sure if it was the sound of her voice, the way her eyes lit up when she talked, or my wanton need to sever her fucking head from her neck that kept me coming back to her.

I don't really remember what she looks like. If her eyes are black, blue, green, or brown. If her hair is black, silver, brown, or red. Her face presents itself as a blank slate each time we meet, and I'm tasked with putting the pieces together.

It's a thought that keeps me awake at night. Not that I'm one for sleeping much, as I've said. I won't take her head like I had done with the others. I won't be frantic about it; I won't be sloppy about it.

I'm not a messy man.

I keep a room refrigerated for things of this nature. The cool air keeps me happy, and the warmth of the blood when it splatters against me is very arousing. The sound of the little drips and drops when I'm done and the screaming is over, are so captivating. A secret melody that only I can witness as they greet Death in the afterlife and are fucked horribly by whatever demons await them.

I try not to have sex with them.

Sex isn't the point, but sometimes when I'm standing there watching the blood drip from the gaping wound, I can't help myself. The most I've done so far is slide my cock into a hollowed out hole that I've made in the neck. It wasn't for sexual gratification. It was because of a boyish need to know what the blood, bone, and sinew felt like against my skin. A self-discovery of myself, one could argue.

I haven't done it again.

I want that to be perfectly clear.

There are other holes that I won't have to hollow out when I bring her here, and I haven't decided yet if I'll fuck her when she's still alive, or if I would do it at all.

There are a lot of things I haven't decided when it comes to her. The only thing I know for sure is that I'll make a grand masterpiece of her, and she'll be happy here. She won't have a say in the matter, of course, but I want to make sure that she understands fully why she's being displayed when the time comes.

She'll discover that there's more to life than the mundane, everyday nine-to-five jobs that drain so many people. She'll find out that living paycheck to paycheck, drowning in debt, wondering where the next meal would come from isn't something that should have to plague anyone.

I'll take away every fear that I know is lurking inside of her and in the act, I will rid myself of the thoughts that often take over me in the quiet moments I have to myself. The ones that threaten to steal my sanity if I stay still long enough to listen to them.

I am stronger than my thoughts, and I have to find her soon or be relegated to a weeping, insipid human being in the corner of my home behind bricks, wasting away, and waiting for Hell to come and swallow me whole.

CHAPTER TWO

I've put the rag away now, under the sink with the stain cleaner where it belongs. I've gotten dressed and am ready to roam the streets to find her, but as I hover in front of my front door, I feel like something is missing.

I think I know what it is. Maybe today isn't the day to look for her, maybe what I need today is some pain, and I know just where to go. I don't know if I'll get what I need this time, what I feel I deserve, but I'll try it again. One of my best facets is that I don't feel fear. I mean I do, but it's such a rare occasion for me to feel *anything* that I welcome the moments when I can put myself in danger.

As I walk out the front door of my home, I reach into my front shirt pocket and pull out my half smoked pack of cigarettes. I know what you're thinking; if I'm so hell-bent on keeping the shit I put into my body to a minimum, then why do I smoke?

It's a simple, quick satisfaction.

That's all I can really say about it. I'm sure I can stop anytime I want to, much like taking skulls, but I like to enjoy a cigarette every now and then. For instance, this pack has lasted me three weeks. I don't smoke much, I find the taste unsavory and the scent it leaves on my clothing is enough to turn my stomach, but I'm very good about finding things to keep me calm. This just happens to be one of them, so allow me this moment, please.

The end of the cigarette burns brightly as the death hidden so neatly inside of the tightly manufactured paper catches fire, and I inhale deeply. The burning smoke that travels down my throat and into my lungs, blackening them slowly, mummifying them with invisible and hollow fingers, sends a shiver through me. I always feel that way when I haven't had one in a while. I don't know if it's because I can feel myself becoming a living sarcophagus or if it's because I just don't care. But what I do know is that it's that simple, quick satisfaction that I've already explained, that makes all of the damage worth it.

It may be a selfish thought to have, but I'm entitled to selfish moments just like anyone else. And as I walk quickly along the pavement toward my destination, I wonder if maybe I'm not as hideously minded as I'm led to think I am. No one is appealing to my eyes today, which means they're all safe. I can usually find something about anyone that would make me want to bring them home to entertain me for a few hours.

Not today, though.

Today is a day for some much needed pain. It's a day to *feel* without the usual irascible thoughts that would taunt me for not having my main display piece yet.

Pain is a beautiful thing.

It jars all of the senses and brings to life things inside one's self that you didn't know were already there. It lurks, waiting for a chance to come to the surface; pain is a great equalizer. Some can sustain more than others, and those are the ones I like the most. The ones that can last longer before they've reached their breaking point. The ones that bite their lips until they're raw and bleeding, tears streaming down their faces, until they finally submit to the bliss of pain.

It's a lovely, cool day in Kalispell, Montana today. I chose this place purposely because the temperature would drop drastically in the winter meaning I could work outside instead of my home if I wanted to.

I haven't had the chance to do it yet.

One of the most cherished places for me here is a chalet-style mansion on the edge of town. It teeters near Glacier National Park, but it's not easily accessible. It's a hidden mecca of tears, blood, and the occasional exquisite death hiding in plain sight.

Most of the people fear me there. My brand of pain is different than what they've experienced or have witnessed before, but the truly brave ones always rise to the challenge for me.

Most, but not all.

I reach the intersection in the center of town and feel a strong wave of confusion wash over me. How did I get here? This isn't the direction I need to go in, but yet here I am.

My body betrayed my mind again and went off on its own, but this time I was lucky enough to stop myself before doing something quite regrettable in public. Something that would embarrass me enough to stay home for the next solid month.

Putting the cigarette to my lips, I glance around curiously. What was it that brought me here? My thoughts were focused, and I had a purpose, but I lost my way.

Why is it always so easy for me to lose my way?

I'm not lost.

I know exactly where I am now. I let the cigarette slip between my lips and inhale the sweet throngs of hollow death into my rotting lungs and smile briefly. This is exactly where I was a few months ago. It was where I found a street peddler that called himself Monet.

He so desperately wanted to be a piece of art that he compromised himself and used a name that didn't belong to him. I did give him some money though; a twenty-dollar bill if you must know. Then I took him home. I promised him food, a place to sleep, and presented it with the kindest smile I could bring across my face.

My smile makes people trust me.

It's tragic sometimes.

Now that I know why my body brought me here, I go over to the spot outside of the small mom and pop store that he would sit outside of with his sign and sit down. I wonder how easily it would be to be able to swindle people out of money.

You see, I quickly learned that Monet wasn't as destitute as he presented himself. No, he told me that he was too tired to work ten-hour days anymore, and that he knew that three out of five people would find it in their hearts to give him their hard-earned money.

As I bring my knees up to my chest, I chuckle. I understood his meaning, but I didn't appreciate his candor. So when the time came to put an end to Monet's simple life, I was sure to cut out his own heart and give it to him, like so many others had given theirs.

I took my money back after that and went to a local Salvation Army bell ringer and dropped it into their old, red metal basket.

I take another pull of my cigarette realizing I am near the filter and decide to play a game. I look up and down the street before I flick what is left of the paper into the street and ruffle my hair violently. Then I wrap my arms around my knees and look up at everyone that passes me with big, sad eyes.

Will I say anything to them? No, they don't need to hear my words, and I don't need a sign either. My false sadness, my forced tears should be enough to garner some sort of attention.

The first woman; she's large, has brown hair pulled back in a loose bun, and a horrid amount of makeup smeared on her face, but she leans down and gives me a dollar.

I wipe a tear away and nod.

This is too easy.

I wait until she disappears down the street before I get back to my feet, smooth my hair out, and walk into the shop. I quickly locate a package of gum and take it to the counter. With the woman's dollar, I pay for the spearmint flavored breath cleanser, and tell the elderly woman behind the counter to keep the change.

I need to get the taste of this cigarette out of my mouth. It's making me insane and I'm *not* crazy.

As soon as I walk out of the store, I use my teeth to rip away the edge of the gum package. One last look up and down the street is all I need as I pop a piece of gum in my mouth.

I almost lost myself for a moment there.

But my will is strong, and my intentions will get me to where I need to go.

Back on track, toward the pain I need so desperately.

CHAPTER THREE

It doesn't take me long to reach the doors of *La Douleur Folle*. This is my safe place; my home away from home, and one of the few places I like to venture out to when I feel the need for human interaction.

Hm. Not yet.

I walk back down the wooden steps and go around the back of the building. I can hear the sweet serenade inside. Screams of pain, moans of pleasure, and the unmistakable sound of someone being bludgeoned to death.

That was usually a mutual thing

when someone died. However, I could never find satisfaction in someone willing to die at my hands. I enjoyed taking life when it didn't belong willingly to me, and that was what set me apart here. That's what made them fear me, and it's how I know that I can secretly own anyone here I want to.

But she's not here.

I haven't run across her in *La Douleur Folle,* and it's actually a good thing. I wouldn't allow others to touch her or treat her the way they willingly do. She would be mine only, and they would hate me for it. They would wonder why I was keeping such a sweet thing to myself instead of sharing.

It wouldn't be good for either of us, nor for the sanctity of the others here if they attempted to take her from me.

I don't like to kill randomly, but I will if I must. If what I feel is mine is being threatened, I will destroy everything I have to keep it safe.

She's not mine.

For the moment.

I let that thought consume me as I walk the entire length of the building, until I've reached the back, and continue walking toward the property line. It sits on a hill overlooking the state park, and sometimes just being here alone and staring out over creation helps to quiet my urges. Maybe I'd go home today instead of subjecting myself to the need for pain, but it was unlikely. I had already walked so far to get here that I wanted to be compensated in one way or another. Be it in flesh or blood, I wouldn't leave until I felt like the pleasure of my company had been fully paid for.

I stand on the very edge of the mountain, unaware that I haven't yet said that the mansion sits on such. My arms cross loosely over my chest as I look out at the beautiful scenery. I love big sky country; it soothes me and makes me smile.

"I thought that was you," a voice says behind me.

A small smile starts to creep across my lips. I know that voice, it's someone that's always been very kind to me, someone that enjoys when I visit the establishment, because if I'm feeling generous enough, I'll let her watch. We all need to learn how to do these things, and I am an excellent teacher. My methods are my own, and I always make that clear, yet I like knowing that I've helped in some way.

I don't turn around to face her, however she's used to that by now. She knows that I'm not very personable and that I tend to keep to myself, but I indulge her conversations as they come and in turn, she usually leaves me be.

Usually, though not always.

"I was wondering when you would be back. I haven't seen you in a while," she states as she takes a stance next to me.

I glance at her and raise a curious eyebrow. It almost sounds as if she has something for me—a gift—waiting inside.

"I've been busy," I reply.

"Understandable. What brings you back today, Mr. Burress?" she asks with a devilish grin slithering across her thin lips.

It's a putrid smile, reminiscent of a garden snake that's close to death from being left out in the sun too long, and I always have to fight the urge to rip her lips off her face.

"Just in need of some company," I say curtly.

I turn my eyes away from her. She isn't terrible to look at by any means, it's just her smile that turns my stomach. She's asked before to take part in my pain process, but because of that horrendous trait, I always turned her down.

I let her watch, nothing more.

"You came on a good day, then," she responds mysteriously.

"Oh?" I ask, stealing a glance in her direction.

"We have a new member today. She brought her children with her; says that she can't stand living anymore and she doesn't want to see her children in the care of the state. She's looking to go as soon as possible."

"And the children? What am I supposed to do with them?" I ask.

"Whatever your heart desires, Mr. Burress. We aren't equipped to care for children, and she wants them to go with her."

I let out a sigh as I stare out over the park again, letting my eyes drift up toward the now darkening sky. I've never had a child participate in the pain process and I wondered if I would enjoy it.

"How old are the children?" I ask quietly.

"One is fourteen; a terrible mouth

on that girl. She's been nothing but disrespectful since she's arrived," she says, her voice full of disgust.

"And the other?" I press.

She walks around me, teetering on the edge of the mountain and I fight the urge to push her off. That's not who I am though; I don't like to kill unless there's a purpose. I look down at her face, careful not to focus on her lips, and instead search her simmering green eyes. With as much as I hate it, I can tell by the way her eyes crinkle on the sides that she's smiling again. I can't help but let my eyes travel down to her atrocious lips as she forms the words that sets the wheels in motion inside my head; the thoughts that I had spent all day trying to avoid are now becoming louder thinking of those waiting inside.

"Still in the womb."

CHAPTER FOUR

As I walk with Priscilla, the lady of the manor, back up the stairs and into the house, I have a plan already devised. I would do something different today; I would convince the woman inside to live. I would convince her to take her children with her and leave this place because they weren't here for the right reason.

At least not for me.

The child growing inside of her couldn't make the choice to live or die, and that she was taking away that choice and playing God was a bit disconcerting to me.

Why she thought she was allowed to make such a decision in a place such as this, how she even knew how to find it, made me wonder if Priscilla spent too much time with her slimy lips wrapped around the cocks of too many men to have enough common sense to question it.

It's not my place to ask.

We enter into the main room on the ground floor. It's large with high wooden ceilings, low-hanging iron chandeliers, and interestingly enough, a check-in table near the western wall.

I nod quickly at the young, barely legal girl behind the counter. She knows me well by now even though I don't frequent the establishment as much as I used to. She knows to stay far away from a man like me, yet whenever we make eye contact, she always looks at me with seductive eyes, leans over the counter, her large breasts damn near spilling out of her shirt, and gives me a damn charming smile. Maybe I'd find time for her, but for now I am not interested. Especially since she has her long blonde hair pulled back into pig-tails. It makes her look younger than she really is, and I already have enough on my mind when it comes to children.

"Where?" I ask Priscilla.

"I put them in your usual playroom. I figured this would be something you wouldn't pass up," she replies with a chuckle.

I should gut you. I really should rip out your intestines and strew them on the doorway like garland. I should, but I won't.

I nod and walk away from her. I can't let the thoughts consume me. Nothing will get me kicked out this place faster than killing the person that keeps it running. The owner of dark secrets, the purveyor of every dark desire one could imagine, the supplier to our drug of choice;

Priscilla will have to live, or I will lose my sanctuary.

As I climb the main staircase, I can't help but sigh. In my heyday, the entire top floor belonged to me, but as my commitment to this place began to falter, as I came only when I needed to, Priscilla began to give away most of the rooms on my floor. However, the room as soon as I clear the landing is mine. I've done too much, accomplished too many things, for her to give that room away, and she knew it.

I roll my eyes as I put my hand on the doorknob. I can hear them bickering inside; the mother and the teenage daughter. I can hear the daughter telling the mother that she doesn't care what she says, she's not going to die in a place she didn't want to come to.

And that's when I pull the door open.

They both stop their back and forth nonsense and turn their eyes to look at me as I enter. I close the door behind me and turn the lock, but I don't look at them just yet. I find that one of the best feelings in the world is when you gain trust, and to do that I know I have to remove the intentions from my eyes.

Clearing my throat, I walk past them, the mother swollen with her unborn child sitting on the edge of my bed and the teenage daughter standing above her. I keep my eyes low to the black, shag carpet. Priscilla quickly learned that when I needed my doses of pain that blood was usually on the menu, so she replaced the usual white rug with a black one. She said it was more for my protection, so that whoever entered my room wouldn't know how ungodly my desires could be, but, frankly, I think she was just tired of cleaning up my messes.

Not that I minded, because while Priscilla had that hideous mouth, the rest of her could be pleasant on the eyes. If you like that sort of thing, anyway.

I enter the bathroom and close the door behind me. My ritual is always the same. I turn on the faucet and splash hot water onto my face to get my blood flowing. I always pick the soft, white hand-towel second in the stack, and scrub my face vigorously to wake myself up. No matter how ready I always am, I get hit with a sense of tiredness before I begin.

Maybe it's because that's when all sense of humanity in me goes dormant to allow me to act as I truly should, but I can't be sure. And if I'm to be completely honest, I don't care. I know how to snap myself out of it, to bring the evil that harbors the thoughts of madness to the surface, and that's what I need most in these moments.

I place a hand on either side of the skull carved porcelain sink and look into the mirror. My eyes, normally electric blue, are almost completely overcome with their dark center and that's how I know.

It's time.

I place the hand-towel on the side of the sink and turn away from my reflection knowing that I'm a different man now. Knowing that I can commit any atrocity that will satiate my desire as I have so many times before.

It's a powerful feeling and I would be lying if I said that I didn't enjoy it.

As soon as I step back into the room, the girl, with her face twisted in anger and disgust, crosses her arms defiantly over her chest and stares at me. I'm sure the look is meant to make me cower, to second guess my intentions, but it doesn't work, and I smile in place of the fear she was hoping for. A slow, deliberate smile that lets her know who's in control in this room.

"Who the hell are you?" she barks at me.

My eyes leave her face and land

on the mother, who now has her hand resting on her stomach. She's looking at me with pleading eyes, and it only makes my smile widen slightly.

"Do you know why you're in this room?" I ask her softly.

She nods.

I raise an eyebrow. I had expected words because I wanted to know what the sound of her voice sounded like before it was thick with agony.

"And are you sure this is what you want?" I ask, my tone softer than before.

She nods again.

I want to rip her face off; stomp on her neck until her windpipe is crushed for her lack of words, but I control myself.

Self-control is key.

I walk over and sit next to her on the side of the bed. She's too eager for this; too unaware of what comes when partaking in the pain and perhaps ultimately dancing with death.

I have to convince her otherwise,

and when I'm sure she wants to live, I'll kill them all. It's much easier that way and much more enjoyable.

"Then let's begin," I say, rising to my feet.

CHAPTER FIVE

It's no easy feat to convince someone to live when they're truly resigned to death, but I have my ways. A gentle touch coupled with kind words usually does the trick, but this time I have two in my room with only one to convince.

However this scenario will play out, one thing is for certain: I *will* get the pain I came here for today. I walk away from the bed and toward the girl. Her face is no longer twisted in an ugly fashion of anger and false hatred. Now I see a small glimpse of fear.

Good.

"What's your name?" I ask as I take her by the elbow and lead her to a large wooden desk that sits near the French doors. I like the view here, I'm sure I've mentioned that before. It's calming and serene and allows me to enjoy the beauty of nature when I'm in my moments of passion and destruction.

"What do you care?" she spits back as I sit her down firmly in the chair. I chuckle and lean down, placing a hand on the desk, becoming eye level with the girl; a breath away from her face.

"Because I like to know the names of those I'm mourning after they pass," I reply in an even tone.

"You're going to ... kill us?" she asks, her voice breaking slightly.

"I haven't decided yet. I will need your help, and maybe if you assist me, you might be able to walk away from this. A damaged heart, broken will and with, what I would imagine, a mind rotting with what you will witness, but you'll walk away," I reply as I stand back up to my full height.

I watch her cunning eyes as she tries to steal a glance past me. I've purposely blocked her mother from her view, and I think that's the courage she needs to agree to the ultimate betrayal. To take the life of someone who gave it to you is one of the most horrendous atrocities one can commit, but when faced with the prospect of death, I've seen many people agree to terrible things.

Her eyes look up the length of my body slowly, as if she's devouring me standing in front of her, and our eyes meet. She nods just once to let me know that she agrees to the possibility of life, and I hold a hand out to her.

"My name is Verona," she finally relents. "What's yours?"

I can't help but smile. For some reason, her name speaks to me greatly; to the man inside of me, and the maelstrom of evil swirling within.

"Guy Burress," I reply with a slight bow.

"That's funny," she says with a girlish giggle. Finally, I see a glimpse of the child she really is and not the angry woman she's attempting to be.

"How?" I ask, walking her to the bed and setting her down gently next to her mother.

"I don't know. I've never met a guy named Guy before," she replies, a glimmer in her eye and quick shrug to punctuate what she's said.

I nod, the smile leaving my face. I have her where I want her, and I know that with the false promises I've made her she'll do as I ask. But how far is she willing to go to try and win her freedom? Now is the time that I will find out.

"Wait here, Verona. Hold your mother close. Tell her you love her and try to mean it. I know that deep down inside you do; tell her. You'll never get another chance," I say as I turn and walk toward the giant, black armoire that sits on the wall directly across from the bed.

I pull the right door open and then the left. There's no rhyme or reason for it when both doors can be pulled open simultaneously, I just like to do little things to fray the nerves of those watching.

"I haven't heard you yet, Verona," I say sternly as I cross my arms over my chest and look at the array of sharp objects in front of me.

A loud suffering sigh meets my ears, followed by the sound of the bed shuffling slightly. At the very least, I know she has her arms around her mother.

Now you're probably wondering why I'm not spending these moments convincing the mother to live. That should be obvious enough; Verona is doing it for me without knowing it.

I reach forward and slide a finger along the blade of the machete that sits gleaming in the darkness of the armoire. It's beckoning to me to be used; it wants blood, and I will give it more than it could ever want. To begin, I know that the obvious thing I have to do is to cut the unborn child from the mother; it will be the first time I attempt something of that magnitude, and I wonder if I will enjoy it.

It's of no consequence to me—the enjoyment of a task—it's whatever feeds the need inside of me and quiets it long enough that I can go back out and look for her again. I pull the blade off the shelf and hold it up. I can't help but wonder if this is something she would enjoy; watching me as I quell the need for pain. Probably not; this is a lonesome task, but one that I'm damn good at.

I turn to face Mother and Verona. They have their arms wrapped tightly around each other. Verona is running her hand over Mother's hair, and Mother is crying into her shoulder telling her that she's so sorry that it's come to this.

"Come to me," I say loudly enough to startle them both.

Verona looks up at me, then to her mother, then back to me again.

"I don't think she wants this anymore. Can we just go home?" she asks nervously.

"When I'm done. Now come to me. Both of you," I say again as I let the blade swing down to my side.

"But we're going to live, right?" Verona inquires as she gets to her feet and helps her mother to stand.

"For the moment, yes."

CHAPTER SIX

The screams are horrendous when I begin my work. Filled with terror and the knowledge of impending hell waiting to come out of me just for them.

Verona is now in a harness, hanging on the inside of the armoire where she can't get in my way. Where she can't make unnecessarily attempts to save her mother in vain. I will not forget about her. I just want to save her for last.

It's taken nine furious hits with the hilt of the machete to stop Mother from fighting me. Usually those that enter my room are full of fight, and that's what I like the most.

I don't beat women.

This is different.

This is just my way of incapacitating her so that there's a minimal amount of blood to clean up. Priscilla always gets angry when there's a mess, and so do I.

The two of us are on the bed as Verona kicks and screams behind us. She doesn't want her mother to die now, she doesn't hate her, and she never meant anything mean she said to her.

Those are her lies, not mine.

I haven't made any cuts yet. I've simply climbed on top of Mother and ripped her shirt open. She's weak now; hit one too many times with the end of a blunt object, her eyes slowly rolling back and forth as my hand caresses her stomach.

"Is it a boy or a girl?" I ask her.

"Leave her alone you motherfucking piece of shit!" Verona screams from behind me.

I roll my eyes and shake my head; I'll be sure to cut her tongue out by the time I am done in this room. Perhaps I'll let her live with a gaping wound in her mouth so she will learn how to speak to others with respect.

Perhaps, but not likely.

"Uhh..." is all Mother can offer me in response.

"It's okay," I tell her softly, as I lean forward and run a hand gently down the side of her face. "I like surprises."

I move quickly and carefully, sliding the blade as deeply into the lower part of her stomach as I dare. I don't want the child to die in her stomach. I want to see it first, hold it, give it the hope of love, before I rob it of life.

I'm not a thief.

It has no choice in the matter, as I've said, and I just like the thought of being able to look into its face. To watch it as it molds to me for the few moments that I let it live, to let it believe that it's in a warm safe place as I have thought so many times before.

Oh her screams are glorious the harder I pull the blade across! It digs in maybe an inch deeper, and I use both hands to steady it so that it doesn't go any further in than it needs to. Behind me Verona is screaming violent threats of what she'll do to me as soon as she frees herself, but I pay her no mind. This task is meticulous and must be handled with care if I want them both to live.

One could argue that I'm providing a service, or a kindness even. But, of course, that would only be argued by someone that doesn't know me, and I would allow them the thoughts.

"I'm almost done," I say to her through grit teeth as I continue dragging the machete as far inside of her as I dare to go, and across. The sound of the flesh as it rips is almost melodic to me. Chaotic in its tune, but a beautiful sonata, nonetheless.

I'm almost to the other side of her stomach when something inside me snaps and I lose my careful patience. I take a deep breath and place a hand down firmly on her stomach and yank the blade the rest of the way across. One jerk. Two. The blood flowing out of the giant gash on her stomach is majestic and for a moment, I lose myself in the sight.

I had never seen such an amount of blood flow from a body before and I wonder if she would mind terribly if I stuck myself inside of her.

Remove the baby first.

I pull the machete out of her and lay it on the bed next to us. She's too weak now to use it, and even if she tried, I would be able to stop her. I dig my hands into her, as far in as they will go—which turns out to be almost my entire forearms. I'm not sure what I'm supposed to be feeling for, but I know that I've cut her deeply enough when my hands brush against something reminiscent of a newborn child. I turn my head to the side and wrap my hands around it tightly and begin to extract it from her when another song of screams hits my ears.

I look down and smile; it's so small, not full term, but not quite what I would consider premature. I never did ask her how far along she was, but it was of no matter once I had decided on taking the child from her womb.

The umbilical cord is attached to something still inside of her, and I cradle the baby covered in blood and what looks like some kind of mucosal substance against my chest as I tug until it comes out.

Afterbirth? No, this is the placenta.

I lay it on the bed as I hold the baby against me, using my pinkie to let it suckle while it calms.

It's a boy; Verona has a brother.

I gently rock the baby boy in my arms and look up at Verona as she continues to buck like a wild horse.

"PLEASE!" she screams at me through a cascade of tears. "Just let us go!"

"But there *is* nowhere to go," I reply as the little boy's cries begin to subside. "Now, tell me, did your mother pick a name out for the baby?"

Behind me, she moves on the bed, and I reach quickly for the machete. I'm not sure if she had been attempting to wrest it from where it was laying, but I won't allow her the attempt. Not now that my arms are preoccupied with new life.

"Guy, *please!*" she begs.

I chuckle and look down at the little boy still suckling my pinkie and smile. "Are you calm now?"

His eyes, still not open, squeeze together tightly as a small cry escapes from inside of him.

"No?" I ask him softly. I reach for the machete again and place it under the cord, laying it over the blade like a pyramid of sorts. A couple of tugs in a downward manner and I've severed it from the placenta. I get to my feet, machete in one hand, baby in the other arm, and whisper softly to him.

I tell him how the world is a dark place made of utter shit. I tell him of how life isn't really worth living with a mother that wanted him to die and a sister that only thinks of herself. I tell him it's better this way, and I think he believes me.

I lean my face down and press my lips softly against his head for just a moment; to give him the only feeling of love he'll ever know in his short life. Then with his mother watching from the bed, and his sister screaming from her place suspended in the armoire begging me for mercy, begging me for his life, I turn him upside down and grip his ankles.

I smile when I know I have their undivided attention. I raise the baby over my shoulder, the baby boy with no name, and with every bit of strength inside of me, proceed to slam it violently against the wall until the crying stops.

Until there's nothing left but blood, brain matter, and the broken bones of a limp corpse that lived so briefly in a small moment of insincere love.

I take the now mangled shell of a life that was once so briefly and toss it onto the bed with the mother.

"It's a boy."

CHAPTER SEVEN

The inside of my mouth is dry and rotting as I pull on my second cigarette of the day. I'm sure this is some kind of record for me as I'm not much of a smoker. This moment requires a minor sedation, and I happily indulge the need.

But I'm not really happy right now; I'm confused. Confused as to why Verona is still screaming and struggling in the harness. Confused as to how Mother is still alive and not realizing what's happened yet.

Perhaps if I put the baby back inside of her and sew her up somehow, it will be enough of a redeeming act that it won't haunt me for the next few days.

The acts never stayed burned in my mind for too long, but just enough to make me sit and reflect on what I've done. A good man would care, but I'm not a good man.

I have to stop her screaming, it's giving me a headache.

I get to my feet and look around the room. There had to be something I could shove into her mouth that would silence her but not kill her. My plan is to save her for last, so that she can savor the destruction of her family and know that her hatred is what brought them to me.

My eyes drift toward the broken body of the baby boy. I see something just beneath him that I can use. I got to the bed and move his body aside retrieving my new prize and turn toward Verona.

She's screaming louder now that she sees what I'm holding, and I put the cigarette in between my lips. This will have to do.

"Open your mouth, please," I say, now standing in front of her.

"Fuck you!" she screams back, trying to kick me.

"Verona, I need you to stop screaming. Stop fighting the inevitable. You wanted your family dead, didn't you? I saw it in your posture when I first came in, and I obliged. But you have to stop screaming or I'll snap your neck, and that just won't do. Now, please open your mouth," I say tiredly.

She spits on me instead of complying, and as I wipe it off the side of my face, I become ungodly angry. I've never been spit on before, and I don't appreciate the act. I use every ounce of my strength and punch her in the jaw as hard as I can, continuing violently until I hear the snapping sound that tells me that her bone is broken.

"Thank you," I say, as she begins

to cry. In pain, frustration? I don't care; at this point her mouth is hanging open and it's what I needed. Of course, I have to find a way to keep her jaw closed, but that's not going to be a difficult task.

I grunt as I push the bloody placenta into her mouth. Far enough inside to make her gag, but not to obstruct her airway. Choking to death would be too easy, and her little act of defiance has earned her a more glorious death than that.

I use one hand to keep it in place, then reach around her, blindly feeling the shelves in the armoire until my hand closes around a strap of leather. I pull it out and use it to make a tourniquet. It's long enough to wrap around her head at least once, and I step back satisfied that it's done the job quite nicely.

"I imagine that's what a brain with the spine still attached looks like," I muse more to myself than her. Part of the umbilical cord is still attached to the afterbirth and it's swaying softly as she tries to swipe at it.

I raise an eyebrow and watch for a moment. If she pulls it out of her mouth that won't do, but the pain from a broken jaw is restricting her movements, and the most she's been able to do so far is cradle the sides of her face.

"Leave it in," I warn as I pull deeply on the cigarette. "If you pull it out, I'll impale your hands against the door."

Her rage leaves her eyes. It's all replaced by a small, fragile girl terrified of what's unfolding in front of her; resigned to the fate that she so desperately wished secretly upon her mother.

I know girls like Verona; I see them on the streets, and I've had them in my room. In the end, I make them realize that they are worth only the sum of their thoughts. But none of them are ever enough for me because they're not *her*.

Verona begins to gag, and I smile as she brings my attention back to where it belongs—this moment. It snaps me back to the task at hand, and I turn back toward the bed. The boy belongs back inside of his mother; in the warm safe place that so many of us take for granted.

Once we're brought into this world, we're under the weight of our mothers' sins for seven years, then we're on our own. I hadn't afforded him seven minutes before saving him from the hell I knew he had been destined for.

She moans on the bed, her head turning slowly to the right, and I climb on resting next to her. I want her to see my face, my eyes, to remember her last moments with me and no one else. The child will have to wait; this woman has clearly suffered enough in her life that it would be an unnecessary cruelty to sew her child back into her while she was still alive.

I caress the side of her face gently as she blinks slowly. She'll be gone soon enough, and this charade of emotion has to last much longer.

The only sounds in the room are the sounds of Verona whimpering, this dying woman next to me taking slow, shuddering breaths and my own breathing slowing to match hers.

It's a comfort I've learned to give those that don't walk out of my room; to falsify my own death so they don't feel as if they're going into the unknown alone.

She opens her eyes widely and looks into mine one last time, before they shut. Her breathing becomes less and less labored, and I find my hand has moved from her face to her stomach. It's not as firm as it was before, and it's not as majestic when not filled with life, but I gently rub in circular motions.

Death comes to us all.

Is she afraid? Is she accepting of her fate? I don't know. To be honest, I only try to ease her passing as a solace more to myself than her. It quiets the demons that try to revive themselves after the deeds are done.

One last warm breath against the side of my face and she's no more.

I gently lean forward and kiss her forehead before I move myself up to a seated position. Verona is still now, weeping genuine tears as she realizes what's happened.

But does she cry for her family or for herself? A child such as herself would surely not feel any pain at the passing of her mother and brother, would she?

"Look away," I say to her as I get to my feet. I wait until she closes her eyes tightly and reach for the baby boy.

With a deep breath, I pull open the massive wound in their mother's abdomen and begin to cram him back inside of her. I don't care if he's comfortable or if I'm putting him back in the right place, so long as he's inside of her where he belongs. They'll be buried together; I'll make sure of it with Priscilla.

CHAPTER EIGHT

I seem to have a bit of a smoking problem today.

I have my third cigarette hanging from my mouth as I meticulously attempt to sew Verona's mother back to her former state. I don't want there to be a scar, though I know that's a lost cause. If I had cut her correctly when I took the boy out, then there would have been less of a chance, but I lost myself in that moment.

It was of no consequence, I just needed to finish the job. I'm halfway done now, but the damn baby's foot keeps falling back out of the wound prohibiting me from continuing. I don't want to have to sever the leg, but I will if I must.

I give him one last hope to stay whole as I lean down and push him back in, further up into her, causing a rigid bump to form on top of her stomach.

Not my best work, but it will half to do.

I let out a sigh as ash falls from the end of the cigarette onto her stomach. I'm not upset by any means, just relieved that it's over now. He gets to keep his leg, and I'm proud of myself for not following through on that thought.

I sit down on the bed, rub the back of my hand against my forehead, and take the cigarette from my mouth. The oddly shaped mound sitting next to me is watching me. I can see it from the corner of my eye; taunting me, telling me that I haven't done a good job. Telling me to rip him out and start again.

I won't do it.

I won't listen.

I won't let the boy mock me from inside of her.

With a quick, strong shove, I push her body onto the floor on the other side of the bed where I can't see them anymore. Where he can't see me or watch me or provoke me to start over.

I should probably try for that pain now.

"Verona, have you ever been to the circus? Or a carnival?" I ask, glancing up at her.

Her eyes are still closed, her chin is still resting against her chest, and for a moment I fear that I'm speaking to myself, when she coughs quietly.

"Have you?" I ask again.

Her head moves slowly from right to left.

"I used to love going to them when I was a child," I say to her fondly. *Inhale deeply. Hold the smoke. Let it out.* "My favorite performers were the ones that dealt with fire. I don't know why, but I've always found fire to be intoxicating. Before you ask, I'm not a pyromaniac, I just happen to enjoy the colors and the heat."

Her eyes slowly open as she looks up at me, but I don't meet her eyes. I can't; not after what I've done to her family.

"One night I went to a carnival alone. I was about your age, fourteen or fifteen. Anyway," I stop to flick the ashes off the end of the cigarette before I proceed, "there was a performer there that lit his body on fire as part of his act. I was so entranced that I came back every night that they were in town and watched him, trying to figure out what his secret was. I could never quite place what he was doing to be able to walk in the flames, so I stayed the last night they were in town and I asked him. It was my last chance to know his secret."

I steal a glance at her. I want to

know if she's responding to my story, and from what I can tell she is. It would be a much more pleasant conversation if I could remove the waste-filled sac from her mouth, but her form of participation is screaming, and I finally got the headaches to secede.

"It took some convincing until I finally got him to reveal his secret. He had a coat of fire-retardant gel on his skin. A thin enough layer that the crowd wouldn't notice, yet thick enough to keep him from being burned to death. How his organs survived the smoke inhalation is another matter, yet the thought never came across as thought in my mind until I became an adult. But this is only the second time I've ever wondered it, so as you can imagine, that part was never really important to me."

I stand up and walk to the desk, snuffing the cigarette out in the ashtray. I've forgotten that it's there because I'm not a smoker; I don't need an ashtray. Just inside the armoire is what I need; it'll show her that I've learned the trick and allow me the modicum of pain that would be sufficient enough when coupled with the carnage.

I walk over to her, careful not to meet her eyes, but her body starts to shake. I don't understand why she's so afraid of me. This didn't have to go this far had she not been such a defiant child. Had she obeyed her mother and cared about her family, they never would have found their way to *La Douleur Folle*.

This is strictly her fault. Not mine. I want that to be understood. I could find much better things to do with my time than to slaughter a small family.

Which reminds me.

"I'm not exactly sure what he used, because he wouldn't tell me more than what the trick actually was," I say as I pull a cylindrical tube out of the armoire, "but I'm pretty certain it's something close to this."

I hold it up for her to see, but she doesn't turn her head. I know this because the cord hasn't swayed in the slightest.

I sigh.

"I'm going to do something special just for you, and I'd like you to watch me please," I say to her in a soft, but stern tone. "Can you do that Verona?"

"Mph."

I accept that as a yes and reach for the small butane lighter that sat next to the tube. A shiver quickly shoots through my body as I try to mentally prepare myself; to make sure that I don't forget to put the gel on first.

I crack my neck to the right, and a small pop meets my ears. I'm ready now. I go back to the desk and place my items down before I begin.

I pull my shirt off and the cord swings gently. I can see it as I raise my eyes quickly toward her. I know that she'll appreciate my body and more than likely, what I have planned to show her.

I continue to undress, unbuckling my belt, undoing the zipper in my jeans, pushing them off, and stepping out of them.

The cord swings again, and I swear to God I'm almost sure I can smell her now. She's aroused at the sight of me in my almost nakedness, but I push that thought away. I won't fuck a child; and even if I ever found it in myself to do it, it certainly wouldn't be this one.

"Are you watching?" I ask quietly, placing my thumbs on the inside of the waistband in my boxers.

"Mph."

I pull them off and step out of them. I use my foot to kick my clothes away then reach for the tube of gel. I wonder if it's cold, warm, what it will feel like, or if it will protect me. So I decide that instead of my entire body, I'll just light a part of me on fire. It should be a grand spectacle, and if it goes wrong, I have other ways of fucking. It wouldn't make me any less of a man.

I'm becoming hard now. I can feel the blood causing me to rise in my own hand, the more I rub the gel on my shaft and over the head, making sure that everything is properly covered.

It's an embarrassment. That my own hands can cause me to become aroused doesn't say much about me, but I chalk it up to the nerve endings and decide to ignore it.

"I'm ready. Are you?" I ask, finally looking up and meeting her eyes. She's watching me; her eyes wide, curious, and full of sinful intent. But as I reach for the torch, I know that in a matter of mere moments she'll think much differently of me.

Except I can't get the smell of her out of my nose; it's inhabiting my senses, playing with my demons, trying to make me do things I refuse to do.

I know how to stop this.

I turn the torch on.

I lower it to my hard cock, and I run the burning flame up and down, over, and over, closer, and closer, until I grit my teeth. Until I feel the pain I was craving so deeply.

Until I can pull the torch away and stand there looking down, completely mesmerized as the fire burns down below, hoping against hope that I'll be able to snap out of this trance before it's too late.

CHAPTER NINE

I'm frantic.

I expected a burn, a singe, the smell of flesh set alight, but nothing. Not even the pain I wanted to feel is present after I snuff the small fire out.

What have I done to myself that I can't feel pain anymore? The exquisite release; the one thing that made me identify with being an actual person seems to have vanished.

If I can't feel it anymore, then I'll watch it.

I quickly walk toward the door and pull it open. Walking toward the side railing, I lean over slightly searching for someone, anyone that would be a willing participant in what I now have in mind.

Fuck.

I put two fingers to my lips and let out a shrill whistle to get her attention. It's the young woman with the pigtails; the only one visible on the lower floor whose attention I want.

She jumps, obviously startled by the sudden sound, and looks up at me. The smile on her face is because she's regarding my naked physique, but I couldn't care less. I know she wants to fuck me; her eyes tell me as such each time I come in here. I also know that she's so lost in the delusion that it *could* happen, that she'll be willing to do whatever I ask her to.

"Hi!" she calls up to me cheerfully. I assume it to be cheerful because if it was meant to be a seductive tone, it failed miserably.

"Would you like to come into my

room?" I ask, crossing my arms over the side railing.

Her eyes widen at the prospect, and I'm sure there's a pool forming on the chair she's sitting in. I don't care; whatever gets her into my room, regardless of the false promises she seems to think my being stark naked on the landing is providing.

"Am I allowed to?" she asks, her eyes widening even further still. It makes me wonder about the structure of her skull; how deeply her sockets go that she can widen her eyes so greatly.

"For tonight," I reply, a small smile starting to cross my lips. It's somewhat genuine, in I know what will happen once I close the door behind her, yet somewhat forced in the essence of seduction. My words won't be enough to sway her from her place at the desk, but if I smile, act like I really want her company, she will oblige me.

And it works.

I wait as she pushes her chair away from her desk. I lean against the railing and force myself not to roll my eyes as she starts bounding up the stairs like an eager child.

I've had enough of children today.

This is why I need her.

"What's your name?" I ask her as she reaches the top stair.

"Honey," she replies, her eyes half closing, her voice thick with another failed attempt at seducing me.

"Your real name," I reply evenly.

"Laura," she says as she flips one of her pigtails behind her shoulder. She walks onto the landing closer to me, and I try my damnedest not to cringe as she wraps her arms around my waist.

"What can I do for you?" she asks, attempting to lean in closer to my face.

I gently put my hands on her wrists and undo her grip. I fight with myself not to snap them and throw her over the railing. Instead, I force the smile back onto my face and I look down into her doe-shaped eyes.

"I want to watch."

CHAPTER TEN

As soon as I close the door firmly behind us, Laura realizes the error in allowing her lust for me to compromise her better judgment.

But once someone enters my room, they don't leave until my terms have been satisfied and fulfilled.

"What ... what do you want me to do?" she asks, her eyes darting between the legs on the floor, the young girl hanging on the door of the armoire, and me.

"I seem to have lost something, so I'd like you to help me get it back.

Verona here will help us, won't you?" I ask, glancing at her.

Her eyes cut toward me quickly, then to the lifeless body of her mother, and a fresh stream of tears is her only answer.

"Um, I'm not really into the bi thing," Laura says to me as she attempts to inch backward toward the door.

"Today you are," I reply, gripping her by the arm firmly and walking her toward Verona. "I'm going to take this out of your mouth now. If you scream, I slit your throat, understood?"

Verona whimpers, but nods in agreement. I have finally managed to rid myself of a head full of her screams, and I don't care to hear them resume.

I remove the emptying sac from her mouth and toss it to the side. I lean close enough to inspect her lips. There is a thin film that gently coats them, and I turn toward Laura beckoning her toward us.

"In the bathroom there are hand towels. Run one under warm water then wash her face, please. She shouldn't have to be used with a dirty face. It's unbecoming."

Laura is starting to shake. I can feel it, sense it almost, as she walks slowly toward the bathroom. In a matter of moments, I hear the faucets turn on and off. She reappears, towel in hand, and gently wipes Verona's lips clean.

"I should probably go back down to the desk. Priscilla will be angry if she sees that I'm not there," she says in a soft, shaky voice.

"Priscilla knows that the only person you would leave for is me; as I also know. I've seen the way you look at me when I enter this place. I've felt your eyes bore into me as I walk up to my room. I know you want to please me, Laura. This is how you will do it," I reply as I walk toward the pile of clothes on the carpet.

"Well, what do I get for doing

this? From you?" she asks, turning to face me.

"Knowing that I'm satisfied with a well done job and a possible place in my room in the future," I reply as I pull my shirt over my head.

I know that for most people that wouldn't mean much, but to this insipid girl with the starry eyes, it means the world.

"Promise?" she asks quietly.

"I guarantee it," I reply with a smile. I hide the sinister intentions well within it, not wanting to scare her out of this moment. I reach down for my underwear and pull them on, followed quickly by my jeans.

"Okay. What do you need me to do?" she asks.

"In the armoire," I say as I zip my jeans, "there's a very special strap-on I had made a few years ago. I've only ever seen it used once, maybe twice, none of the times seem to stick because none of them were special enough to stay with me. Anyway, I'd like you to undress and then pull it on."

Laura looks at me wearily before she reaches past Verona, who seems to have joined in the symphony of trembling bodies and begins to ruffle around. She'll know it when she sees it; it's quite a masterpiece, and while I had been saving it until I came across *her* again, I would most definitely enjoy seeing it used right now.

"Oh my God," she says in a shell-shocked tone. I cross my arms over my chest as a half-cocked smile dances across my lips. Her reaction makes it clearly obvious that she's found what I want her to wear.

"There's no way I can fucking do this. Not if it's what I think you want me to do," she says, pulling it out and turning to face me.

"Yes, you fucking will because it *is* what I want. You want to satisfy me? You crave me, you want me inside of you, fucking you mercilessly until you scream in ecstasy, correct?

Then take your fucking clothes off and put it on."

I walk purposefully toward both of the young women and undo the straps around Verona's body. I pull her up and out of the harness and hold her closely as her body collapses against mine.

It's exhaustion.

I've felt that before.

"It'll all be over soon, then you'll get to be with your mother and brother," I say softly to her as I lay her on the bed.

I turn toward Laura who's now securing the special piece into place. I let out a happy sigh and smile like a hopeless fool. In the dim light of the room, the artistry is hard to see, but it's so fucking special. And when covered with blood, it's downright majestic.

Like her skull will be when in its rightful place.

Laura walks toward me, wiping tears away from her face. She's not built for this; she's one of the people that comes here that likes to pretend they know pain; they *know* the joy of feeling it and inflicting it, but when faced with the prospect, show their true cowardice.

I sit on the bed next to Verona as Laura stands at the edge.

"Are you ready?" I ask her.

She nods, though her tears tell me otherwise. I look down at the twelve inch, thick, serrated knife that stands in the place of where a false dick should be and wait for Laura to begin.

CHAPTER ELEVEN

"His name is Joseph."

I've already decided, but as I watch Laura begin to climb onto the bed, ready to give pleasure to my eyes, I stop her.

Verona's head is lying in my lap as I hold the sides of her face gently. I'd almost forgotten she was here. Had I not thought to name the boy, I would have missed the moment to ask her.

"Do you think he would like that name?" I ask thoughtfully, glancing down into her eyes.

The stains of old tears and regret stream down the sides of her face, gently rolling against my thumbs. New tears, fresh with silent pleas and thoughtless hope replace them.

"He looked like a Joseph," I say more to myself than her.

Verona is sobbing so heavily that I know she can't answer me. She probably doesn't know what I'm talking about and to be quite honest, had I been in her position I wouldn't have known either.

But I'm not.

"Don't cry. I won't let you feel it for very long," I promise as I raise my eyes toward Laura and give her a nod. "Proceed."

My eyes drift down Verona's trembling body as Laura grips her sides firmly. Both are looking at me; begging me to end this before it begins, but we've already come this far.

"Do it," I say to Laura in a stern tone.

Verona's sobs turn to wails, then are promptly followed by screams as

Laura starts to insert the devious device of sexual gratification inside of her. I close my eyes tightly and listen closely. You can always hear the first rip if you really want to; you just need to drown out the world around you and open your soul to the beautiful sound of tearing flesh.

I smile and my head tilts to the right. There it is; it may not have been the first, it may not have been the second, but I'm still able to hear the skin as it tears, the rushing sound of warm blood, and the purely erotic thrusts that are now rapidly happening.

I know what Laura is doing.

She wants her to bleed out, she wants her to die quickly, and while I would prefer it to stretch out, I'm inclined to agree.

I firmly put my hand over Verona's mouth. Her screams are starting to jar my nerves, and I can feel another headache quickly coming on. She bares her teeth and attempts to bite me, which makes me look down at her and smile.

She has more fight in her than I had anticipated.

"Shh ..." I whisper as I place the palm of my other hand over her nose and press down firmly.

Her body becomes frantic with fear. It's losing oxygen and being shredded from the inside, and it doesn't know how to protect itself. One hand is attacking mine, one hand is shoving viciously at Laura, but neither of us relent. I refuse to, and Laura—well, she's been misled by false promises that I have no intention of following through on.

It takes the body approximately three minutes to die when it's cut off from one of its major life sustaining sources; in this instance, it's air. The lungs, from what I understand, feel like they're on fire and it's a very intimate way to die.

Verona has lost consciousness. I look down toward Laura. The blade is thick with blood and tissue, and now that there are no screams to contend with, I can hear the melodic tune of debridement.

It's a beautiful massacre, and I know that I won't ever be able to forget this moment.

A quick glance down at Verona's chest shows me that she's slowing down. Her life is draining from her, most likely because of the suffocation, but I'll let Laura believe that she granted her mercy by fucking her faster than I wanted her to. I'll let her believe that in all of the blood and madness, that she did a good thing.

Another minute ticks by. Laura is getting tired, Verona is almost cold, but I enjoy watching, so I don't tell her that she's left us already. Instead, I let her continue for another thirty seconds, before I wave her back.

"Enough. It's over," I say quietly.

"Get this fucking thing off of me!" she screams as she frantically starts to undo the straps.

"Did you enjoy it?" I ask her curiously as I run my hands over Verona's hair.

"No, I didn't fucking enjoy it!" she shrieks at me. "You're completely sick! You're crazy!"

And that's all it takes really.

I move Verona's head gently off of my lap and kiss her forehead. I climb off of the side of the bed and walk toward the end where Laura stands, arms wrapped around herself, and body shaking terribly.

I reach down for the device from where she's dropped it on the ground and stand quickly. A handful of her hair is now wrapped around my fist.

"I'm *not* crazy," I reply calmly as I ram the soiled blade down her throat.

CHAPTER TWELVE

My hands are folded behind my head as I lay on my bed. It took me about twenty minutes to get back home—much faster than it took to get there—and I'm taking the time to reflect on what I saw moments ago.

Priscilla is angry with me. Not for what I've done to Verona, Joseph, and their mother, but for what I've done to Laura. She scolded me like a child, telling me it's hard to find trustworthy people to work for her and that it had taken her about a year to find Laura.

I promised her compensation before I left in any manner she

wanted, which she promptly took me up on. I still feel dirty from how quickly she dropped onto her knees, wrapped her slimy lips around my cock, and sucked until I exploded in her mouth.

I did it as fast as I could. Normally, I enjoy little sexually gratifying things like that, but not from her.

Not ever from her.

I decided as soon as I got home that it would most likely be years before I'd go back. The shame of letting her touch me in the way that she did to pay off a debt that really shouldn't have been mine to bear, completely fucked with my head and I hated it.

So, as I lay here, I close my eyes and attempt to keep those thoughts away. I want to fill my head with the artistry of a slaughtered family. The birth of a beautiful child that I was able to hold for a few moments, and the end of a girl that held no love in her heart for anyone other than herself.

Verona's screams will stay with me for a while, but I can always take solace in knowing that Joseph went into the afterlife loved and with a name. I can assure myself that I fulfilled the mother's wishes and gave her what she wanted; an exquisite death.

I run my hand roughly over my face. I can't get the thought of Priscilla, or the feel of her mouth wrapped around me to secede. Maybe I should begin with the bricks now. Maybe I should just give up my hopes of finding *her*.

But I can't and I won't.

Not yet.

The time hasn't come to wall myself into my home with my collection of skulls. It wouldn't come until I was able to bring her in and make her my masterpiece. But the thoughts ... they won't stop. They tell me that the world will be safer when I decide to stop myself. They tell me that she'll reject me, and that if she trusted me, I would already have her here.

Trust is fragile.

My eyes open and I sit up. There has to be some way to get her to trust me. There has to be something I can do to prove to her that I'm not an ordinary man and that she would enjoy more than the small conversations we have when we see each other.

With a frustrated grunt, I reach into my front pocket and pull out another cigarette. If this continues, I'll become a regular smoker, and I'll be forced to remove my own lungs before cancer forms to stop me.

But that would take years.

It won't take me that long to find her. I just have to go out and look for her. I try to remember where I last saw her, and I'm pretty sure it was at the small organic grocery store near the strip mall.

It makes me smile that she likes to eat healthy; she takes care of her body like I do. I ignore the fact that she had a brown fast food bag in the front seat of her car when she pulled away because it doesn't make sense to me.

I need things to make sense.

Inhaling deeply, I pull my legs up to my chest and rest my arms over my knees. I try to focus on the rushing sound of blood that poured so freely from Verona.

Was she a virgin?

Probably not; a girl with a mouth like that, with total disregard for her family had most likely taken a cock or two in her day. Most likely at the same time.

I should probably try to get some sleep. Maybe if I close my eyes long enough and let the visual stimulation wash over me in the darkness, when I wake up this evening the world will seem safer.

Things might make more sense, and I can go hunting again. I can go out and find her and somehow convince her that the safest place in the world is with me.

I can put her where she belongs, and I can stop the ever-swirling, maddening thoughts that fill me every day. I can be normal again, and once I've made sure that I finally have everything I've ever wanted, the bricks will go up.

One by one.

Until even the sun refuses to look at me anymore.

CHAPTER THIRTEEN

Somewhere in my home there's a phone ringing. I rarely make contact with the outside world unless I purposely choose to leave my home, so I always forget that I have one.

And if I don't get off of this fucking bed and find it, it will send me into one of my frantic states. It's bad enough that I'm already fighting a spell from being awoken so rudely by the shrill sound, to lose myself into the madness so quickly wouldn't serve to do anything but keep me locked in my home for an ungodly amount of time.

Time is not something I care to wager on; not when there's so much at stake. Not when there's a world to save, a skull to take, and a tomb to encase myself in.

Where the fuck did I put the damn thing? I'm getting closer because the ringing is becoming louder the more I walk through my home, but I have no idea where one would even put a phone they rarely use.

Standing in the doorway of my living room, I look around and sigh heavily. Usually, I'm not one to quit anything, but when I realize that I had apparently turned on the television on the way to my room, for whatever reason, I find my enigma has resolved itself.

I walk in and grab the remote control from the coffee table and use the power button to turn it off before I sit in my usual place on the couch. The place where I can look at my accomplishments thus far and reflect on what I've done, and hope for the possible future ahead of me.

I'm becoming frustrated and that won't do. I just need to sit here, relax, and look at cabinet. I need to focus on what I know I'm capable of doing and just do it.

I'm almost in my zone when there's a knock on the door. Who the fuck could that possibly be? No one I know ever comes to see me, not that I know many people who can tolerate being around me for too long.

Most of them think my cabinet houses macabre props and for the most part, they don't ask questions. I haven't seen my mother in years and I'm not exactly sure who my father is; not that I care.

Actually, now that the thought is walking quietly through my mind, I'm pretty sure I have an idea who he is, but that serves no purpose to me, so I leave it be.

The knock comes again, louder this time; more persistent in its rhythm and I stop walking.

I don't like to be rushed.

Whoever is on the other side of the door will now have to wait an extra ten seconds.

Patience is a virtue.

I possess the virtue of patience, and I expect those that wish to be near me to have the same. Once I've counted to ten, I proceed walking toward the door. I could glance out the side curtain to see who it is, but as I've stated before, I like surprises.

I wonder who it is.

I pull the door open quickly and groan inwardly. It's Priscilla. I don't want to know why she's here, because if she's come for another go at sucking my cock, I'm going to snap, take her skull, and crush it under a hammer. I didn't want her in my home, let alone in my cabinet.

"What are you doing here?" I ask,

stepping out and blocking the doorway.

"I was debating about whether I should come here at all," she starts slowly and so quietly that I almost lean forward to hear her better.

"Okay. So why are you here?" I repeat.

"I have a bill. For what it will cost to clean your room after what you did in there. I didn't know the extent of it until I walked in, Mr. Burress. It looked like an animal had mauled them to death," she said, her eyes darting up into mine nervously.

"I've already paid you," I replied through grit teeth.

Deep breath in. And out.

In.

And out.

"That wasn't enough. Not nearly enough for what you did to that poor family," she says as she takes a step back and darts her serpentine tongue over her thin, slimy lips.

It takes me a moment to control

myself. It takes two more to keep myself from cringing and remembering how late last night, that mouth I detested so much had been wrapped around my dick sucking vigorously.

"Just give me the amount and I'll come by later and pay it," I reply irritably. I had subjected myself to her grotesque mouth for no reason. I'd pay her alright; in pain and blood.

Priscilla shakes her head sadly. "I not sure that I can allow you back into my establishment, Mr. Burress. It's a shame because you were such a great addition, but if you can't learn to control yourself, I can't let you come back."

I smile.

I had no plans of going back anytime soon, but now she's issued a challenge. One that I'll gladly accept.

"Then allow me to invite you into mine," I reply, turning to the side and gesturing inside my home.

She hesitates, but only for a moment.

As she walks in, I close the door securely behind her, turning the lock into place. I still haven't decided if she'll walk out as she walked in.

Whole.

CHAPTER FOURTEEN

I subdue her almost immediately. I don't appreciate her being here, and I don't think she'll have much to say once I'm done with her anyway. She's already seen what I'm capable of, and what I plan on doing to her will make her too afraid to talk anyway.

I already know how to keep her from screaming, which is always the first task of any burden I undertake. But with Priscilla, it will be much more meaningful.

Her body is not something I care to preserve as I drag her, unconscious, through my home and toward my cellar. I've missed my freezing room, and it only pains me that she's the first to be there in months. That room has only ever been used when I planned on keeping a treasure to place in my cabinet, but it would have to do for now.

While I *have* said that I don't work in my home, or let blood be spilled in it, I don't consider my underground freezer to be part of my home. It's my room to fulfill secret desires that no one else would ever understand and, as such, I have learned to separate the two.

With a sigh, I open the cellar door and roll her body down the stairs. Maybe she'll snap her neck on the way down and save herself some pain. Maybe she won't. Either way, I plan on going through with what's already dancing through my mind.

I pull the door closed behind me as I walk down the wooden steps. I tell myself for the hundredth time that I have to rip the stairs out and replace them with concrete, but I also must find the time to allot for that.

It's definitely not today.

My project is already lying on the dusty cement floor moaning. I roll my eyes as I walk toward the freezer door and use my strength to pry it open. There's a simpler way to do it, I'm sure, but I like to assert my standing as the man of the house in front of whomever is going in. No better way to do that than to show that I'm much stronger than they would most likely assume me to be.

"In you go," I say as I walk over to her crumpled body and lift her up into my arms. I take my steps into the freezer and kick the door closed behind us.

I do hope the door opens when I attempt to leave. I've almost been stuck in here once, but that was because I wasn't careful with how I closed the door; much like I just did now.

I'll worry about that when I am

done with her. Placing her on the cold, steel table, I put my hands on the edge of it and wait for her to come back to the current moment at hand.

I never begin unless they're aware of what's to come. They need to feel every ounce of pain to fully appreciate the art they become, and even though she'll never be a favorite work of mine, she'll be remembered.

They all are.

"Priscilla," I say softly, "It's time to wake up now."

She groans again, her head rolling from right to left. I find myself wondering why they do that. What about pain makes us roll our heads on our necks? Is it a coping mechanism? Is it just something to do? Why does it annoy me so much?

"Priscilla," I say in a sterner voice.

She begins to blink rapidly, trying desperately to focus her eyes. I don't mind waiting, because as I've said, patience is a virtue.

Her eyes squint at the hanging

light above her. I never turn it off, even when I'm done in this room. I like the illumination, and it helps sometimes when I have a headache, as strange as it may sound.

She rolls her head again before finally letting her eyes travel up my body until they reach my face.

"Are you awake now?" I ask gently.

She attempts to sit up and then tries to roll off the side of the table. She doesn't realize that there's nowhere to go. But they all do that.

It's the basic human instinct—to survive.

And it's my basic human instinct to kill that hope as quickly as possible. However, I will allow Priscilla a few moments to try to find her way out of the room.

I have to prepare myself after all.

"I've always hated your mouth," I say as I turn my back to her. Somewhere in this old, wooden tool chest should be some twine. Ah! There it is!

"Your lips remind me of two slugs that have had salt poured onto them and are curling up and dying. Has anyone else ever told you that? How unpleasant your mouth is?" I ask as I continue to look in the tool chest for ...

Got it.

"Mr. Burress! Just tell me what I have to do to get out of here in one piece. I promise I won't go to the police, and I promise I won't tell anyone anything," she tries to bargain.

I chuckle.

They all have bargains.

"You'll live through this if you decide to play along," I reply as I turn around to face her. It takes me a moment to find her cowering in the far left corner and I shake my head.

"Please come back to the table," I request softly. I find that using a kind tone usually helps; not always, but usually.

"What are you going to do to me?" she asks, holding her hands up.

I've never seen a larger display of

cowardice from someone who makes a living on pain. It's starting to frustrate me, but I can control it this time.

"I'm going to help you," I reply simply, setting the twine, the shears, and some gauze on the table. "But you have to come back to me right now before I lose the moment of generosity I'm feeling."

Priscilla gets to her feet. Her eyes are wild as she scans for an escape. I can't fault her. I wouldn't show fear in a moment like this, but she's nothing like me. She's a pretender to pain—a false prophet of unimaginable pleasure.

I'll show her what it's like to worship in a true moment of ecstasy.

CHAPTER FIFTEEN

Fifteen minutes. That's how long it's taken me to coax her to the fucking table, and I'm able to contain my livid feelings quite well. I intend to keep my word and let her live, but there are some alterations that are needed before I let her go, and I will not let her leave until I've been able to make them.

"There you go. Sit on the table facing me, please," I say as patiently as I can. Her lips are trembling; they taunt me as they quiver, and I take pride in knowing that I can control my urge to use the shears to impale her against the table.

It would be an unnecessary thing to do, and I only act out of necessity.

"I want you to know something before I do this," I say to her as I pick up the shears. "I've always had a distaste for what you do. Yes, I enjoy going there from time to time, but to have such intimate and beautifully tortuous moments come with a price tag is uncouth. No one should ever have to pay for experiencing a rapture as such."

"I'm sorry," she says, her lips trembling slightly harder, and I cringe.

"Your apology is well received. Now I need you to do your best not to scream," I reply kindly as I put a hand under her chin. "And try not to move too much; God knows where these will end up if I slip."

A blubbering sob escapes her mouth. I sigh and give her a stern look.

"I'm rather low on twine and don't want to have to sew your lips together. Now please sit still."

Priscilla closes her eyes tightly as I place the shears around the edge of her mouth. It should only take one snip ... Ah! Easier than I thought.

Her lips tumble down her chest and land on her lap—a bloody mess, but at least in their full respectable pieces. You should probably know that they look worse when they're not connected to the rest of her face, but I'll remedy this shortly.

I won't look at her.

Not yet.

I don't want to have nightmares of what a face looks like without lips attached. I imagine the hole that she spews her words out of are now baring her teeth and that's enough for me. Looking at it would only serve to do one of two things: either I would vomit, or I would become engrossed in what she looks like and proceed to flay her.

But Priscilla doesn't deserve that much attention from me, and I won't give it to her.

"I should have put on gloves," I say more to myself than her, with a chuckle. On the spool of twine, there's a thick sewing needle attached. I've used it before and can appreciate the sturdiness of it.

Reaching down for what I'm assuming to be her lower, thin lip, I use two fingers to push it inside out before holding against the macabre spectate in front of me.

This is definitely going to give me nightmares and I don't ever suggest trying it. Of course, that's merely a suggestion. I would never dream of telling another how to work their craft.

She whimpers and grunts. I don't know how those two sounds came out in unison, but that's the only way I can describe it.

"Hold still, now. You're doing so well," I say softly as I begin to sew her lip against her face. I move quickly because the sight of her teeth, now bloody and mocking, are starting to stir the maelstrom in me.

Move faster.

My hands take on a life of their own as I grab her upper lip, turn it inside out, and quickly continue sewing. I step back and look, satisfied that I can't see her teeth anymore, yet disappointed in the immediate swelling.

"Here," I say, stepping toward her again. I pull out the last line of twine, hoping that I have enough, and begin to sew her lips together.

She's whimpering and grunting again, and I grit my teeth. If she doesn't stop making that fucking noise, I'll use the shears to slit her throat, and that just won't do.

"Be quiet," I warn.

Two simple words cause such a change in her. She grips the edge of the table and closes her eyes tightly. She accepts the pain and seemingly understands that she has no place in a world such as mine.

A world of true pain.

A temple filled with sexual deviance, malice, symphonic undertones of death, and melodic hues of euphoria. This is where she failed to worship, and this is now her punishment.

"That should help with the swelling. Don't remove the stitching for about two weeks and you should be okay. Also, I suggest you don't go back to *La Douleur Folle* until you've healed. We wouldn't want you to say anything that you've promised you wouldn't," I say in an even tone.

She nods and lowers herself off of the table. I smile at her, take her by the hand, and lead her toward the door. Luckily, it hadn't locked, so I take it as a sign that Priscilla will honor her end of the bargain.

If she doesn't, I'll know where to find her. I'll show her that what she's experienced today for daring to come to my home with demands is *nothing* compared to the evil within that I fight every day.

The evil that waits for the one that truly deserves it.

CHAPTER SIXTEEN

I have such a peculiar feeling about how the rest of my day will go. I can't quite place the emotion, so peculiar will have to do.

Priscilla's gone now and I'm alone. Nothing inside of me is poking or prodding at me, and I feel something strangely unusual.

I feel calm.

It could very well be the proverbial calm before the storm, but I have nothing left to give really. Not until I find the one that keeps eluding me.

I think I'll spend the rest of my day retracing my steps. Where the hell was the last time that I saw her? The grocery store. What was she wearing? ... I can't remember.

I won't bother trying to recall her face, her eyes, or the color of her hair because it's useless. It's almost as if each time I see her, she's wearing a new face, her hair is different, and my brain refuses to retain what she looked like the time before.

Why is this happening?

It's quite frustrating.

Perhaps I'll go back into the living room and turn the television back on. Perhaps I'll clean my home. Perhaps I'll go back to bed and forget that the world exists, but I know that none of these will be enough to keep my mind preoccupied.

I won't hurt anyone else today; my quota has been met. Verona and her family were way above what I usually do for a day. To be honest, I can keep myself from hurting more people until I find her.

And then I'll stop.

That's when it will all end, and when I'll finally be at peace with everything I've accomplished so far in my life. Which gives me an idea of how to occupy myself for the day.

First, I have to shower. I don't want the folly of what I've done to be so prominent on my hands. Also, I want to get the feeling of Priscilla off of me.

From every part of my body.

I clear my throat as I make my way to my bedroom to retrieve some fresh clothes, then head into my bathroom. I place everything neatly on the edge of the sink before I turn and pull the glass door open. A moment later, I've tested the heat of the water and begin to undress.

I like to use an exfoliating soap scrub. It assures me that all of the dirt I may have accumulated throughout the day has been removed and leaves me feeling quite refreshed. For my hair, I use a rejuvenating shampoo and conditioner for no other reason than to keep my hair shining and healthy.

I'm not vain.

I take pride in my appearance.

After I lather and rinse the shampoo, I use the conditioner next. It's organic, of course, and smells of eucalyptus. While that sets, I reach for my soap scrub and unscrew the top. It, too, smells like eucalyptus, and while I understand that may seem a bit quirky, I find it's much better than reeking of two different scents.

I find it subtle and slightly intoxicating, as do others around me. It's more for those in the pleasure of my company than for myself. I like to make others comfortable when I can.

I smile as I scrub myself. I can feel the soap working quickly, leaving small trails of grain against my skin. I have to take care not to scrub too deeply because I can draw blood on myself with something as simple as this.

I've done it before.

Call it a morbid curiosity that I wanted satisfied.

I wince as the conditioner starts to drip down into my left eye, but I continue scrubbing, leaving my cock for last. I turn and step under the shower stream and shake my hands vigorously before I wash the conditioner out. Once I'm done, I grab blindly for the towel I have draped over the top of the door and dab at my eyes before turning and grabbing the soap scrub again.

Now would be the time that I would wash away Priscilla's shameless and lewd acts against me. While I had allowed it, I still found it to be completely vile to have a woman such as her deem herself worthy of my cock.

I hated myself for letting her do it, and I could tell because I was scrubbing too quickly, too deeply, too violently.

I'm not clean enough. I can feel it.

I jab my fingers into the jar again

and bring out a generous amount of soap and continue scrubbing, but I can't seem to get the horrid sensation of her off of me. It's burned in my fucking brain, and if I don't stop soon ... Is that blood?

Oh, God. It is, but I have to keep scrubbing. I have to get her off of me. I move my hand faster and reach with my other hand for more soap. Why isn't this working? How is it possible that I'm not clean enough yet? Why is my breathing starting to become heavy? Am I ... am I enjoying this? This attempt to wash her away, her memory, her touch, is making my body feel torrid, and I'm becoming hard. I can feel it.

But if I scrub harder, it'll go away ... won't it? The memory of Priscilla, the hard cock, the feeling that I'm about to—

"Fuck!"

My breathing is heavier now and I feel so betrayed by myself as I look down at my hand. There's small amounts of blood from my attempting to clean myself, but there's also a generous amount of cum on them as well.

This really wasn't meant when I said I wanted to get everything off. I didn't mean to.

Can you forgive me?

CHAPTER SEVENTEEN

Unfortunate that I should find myself in the waiting room of the urgent care center near my home. I'm sure it's nothing major, but when I rubbed myself raw, it became an annoyance to put on even my boxers. I'm hoping an easily attainable prescription will do the trick and allow me to continue on with my day.

I chose Kalispell Evermore Clinic for a very particular reason. A friend of hers works here; reception, if I can recall correctly, and sometimes I like to come in with minimal afflictions and chat with her.

It's as close as I can get to my main goal without actually being able to get to her, so I make the most of these visits.

Today is different, though, and in a rather shockingly pleasant way.

"Burress?" a friendly voice calls out.

I glance up toward the source of the sound and find myself smiling. It's her friend, and instead of being behind the desk, she's wearing dark blue scrubs and has a small file in her hand.

"I know you," she greets me with a smile as I walk passed her and wait patiently while she closes the door behind us.

She leads me down a narrow hallway to a room with a number four on the door. I walk toward the sturdy reclining bed and sit down.

I already know the routine.

"Did I say your last name correctly?" she asks kindly as she sits on the small stool across from me.

"Indeed."

She smiles as she crosses one leg over the other and opens the file with my name on it. My fingers drum along my knees as I wait for the usual barrage of answers.

"What brings you in today, Mr. Burress?" she asks, clicking the top of her pen.

"Guy is fine," I say, running a hand back through my hair. "This is actually a bit embarrassing, so please bear with me.

"Well, just remember, I'm not here to judge you. I'm here to help you, as long as you tell me the one hundred percent truth," she replies warmly.

"Oh, you misunderstand," I reply with a chuckle. "The act is not embarrassing, it's that I allowed it to happen that makes it so."

"Okay. So, what happened?" she presses, her smile beginning to falter.

"I went to an establishment that I frequent, and there was a girl there that allowed me to try something I've wanted to try for years," I began, warning myself not to give too much detail. "Anyway, as it turns out, it worked. Only when I was home earlier, showering and trying to get the essence of another woman off of me, I may not have realized that I wasn't exactly healed."

She's staring at me now. Curiosity shows in her eyes, but I know her mind. It's judging me for what I've just said, and I can't blame her.

Vanilla people are very quick to judge what they don't understand.

"Guy, where are you hurt?" she asks curiously.

I sigh and get to my feet, placing my hands on my hips. Should I show her or ask for another in her place? After all, she's almost as good as the one I'm hunting for, but I won't harm her for the simple fact that she helps others. Something I know I could never do or have the want to attempt.

With another loud sigh, I unzip

my jeans and let them fall down to my knees. She's putting on a purple pair of latex gloves while I contemplate pulling my boxers off. Maybe if I just pull it out the opening it won't be so bad, but I know these health physicians want everything as accessible as possible.

I use my thumbs to slide down my underwear as far as mid-thigh then stop. If that's not enough for her to work with then I would just pull everything back up and leave.

"Doesn't that hurt?" she asks in an awed voice as she uses her thumb and forefinger to examine me.

"No. It's more of an annoying feeling that I'd like to subdue if possible," I reply, turning my face away.

"Did you burn yourself?" she asks curiously as she gently raises my cock to view the underneath.

"That was the trick, so to speak," I reply dryly.

"Okay," she says, gently letting me go and turning toward her file. I wait patiently while she scribbles something down. "You can get dressed now."

I pull my clothing quickly back into place. So quickly that I almost end up snaring myself with my zipper, but I manage to avoid another mishap in that area.

"I'm going to give you something for the burns. I'm assuming you've masturbated since it's happened because your skin looks like it's been rubbed raw."

"Unintentionally, but yes, that's correct," I reply, leaning against the bed.

She glances up at me and raises an eyebrow before almost imperceptibility shaking her head and pulling out a prescription pad.

"I'm not really supposed to do this because the doctor is out today, but sometimes we get to play with these," she says happily as she scribbles something down. "I would advise getting this as soon as possible. The faster you start using it, the faster you can get back to whatever it was that brought you here."

"Thank you," I say quietly.

I take the prescription from her and fold it once, then twice, sliding it into my pocket. I'll pick it up on the way home.

For now, I have to make my way to the hardware store and get some supplies.

CHAPTER EIGHTEEN

I really should learn to use my car more often, but I enjoy walking. No amount of strength I've amassed will aide me in bringing all of the items I've just pushed up to the register. I'll ask for a home delivery; it'll make things much simpler.

Do I have my wallet?

A quick brush of the back of my jeans tells me it's in the left pocket, and I breathe a little easier. There's only one person in front of me and I don't mind waiting. After all, he only has two items and is already swiping his method of payment, so it's just a matter of how quickly the computer will charge him and he can be out of my way.

"I'm sorry sir, but you card is declined."

I sigh loudly and reach for my wallet. I lean over my flatbed dolly and swipe my credit card. My card won't be declined; it never is.

"Thank you, young man," he says.

I nod, force a smile, and move my dolly up as soon as he moves out of the way. *Young man.* I hadn't been called that in years, but I'd let him labor under the thought that a "young man" had done a kindness for him, when all I really wanted was for him to get the fuck out of the way with his pride still intact.

The woman behind the counter grabs her wireless scanner and comes around the register. She begins to scan my items; beep, beep, beep, until she's finally confident that she's processed them all.

"I need these delivered to my

home," I tell her, handing her the pre-filled delivery form.

"That'll be an extra seventy-five dollars," she says, reaching for the form.

"I'm aware."

She nods and scans the form, then proceeds to slowly type the information into her system. I can feel myself becoming angry at the slow pace she's working, and that won't do. Instead of letting the anger consume me, I cross my arms over my chest and glance around the store.

And I see her.

I actually fucking see her.

She's walking toward the exit of the store, right passed me as if I don't exist; as if I don't mean anything to her. I convince myself that she just didn't see me and turn my attention back toward the cashier.

"Are we done? Is there anything else you need from me?" I ask urgently.

"Just need you to sign the receipt

once it prints," she replies to a long roll of paper being slowly ejected from the machine.

I know I shouldn't have, but with the amount of frantic impatience that's now swelling inside of me, I lean passed her, rip the paper out of the machine and sign my name at the bottom.

I shove my credit card back into my wallet and move passed the dolly, quickly weaving my way around the sudden wave of customers who seem to have been miraculously all checked out at once.

"Get out of my fucking way," I bark at a mother and her two rowdy children. She gasps, then huffs as if no one has ever said that to her and her small duo of rancid offspring before.

I can see the exit doors; they're a mere few feet away, and I'm so close to speaking with her again. I'll ask her what her name is this time, and I'll tell her mine. I'll retain her fucking face, eyes, hair, lips, *everything*, and refuse to forget it.

However, as soon as I step out into the blaring daylight, I realize I'm too late. After a quick sweep of the entire parking lot I see her getting into her car and closing the door firmly behind her.

I should run up to her; tap on the window and ask her if she remembers me, but that would give the illusion that I'm nothing more than a desperate madman, and I'm not crazy.

For today she wins. I'll stand here outside of the store and watch her drive away. I'll let her leave me and not know what the blur of the woman that walked passed me looks like. I'll forget that she was here and that I was so close to what I've been needing for so long, and I'll be okay with it.

Why? Because I'm coming closer to my grand conclusion. I'm so close that now I know that she drives a blue Chevy Impala, and the license plate number is 574-ECA.

I have more information about her than I would care to admit, and I'll find her soon enough. I'll speak to her, charm her, invite into my home, and she'll accept.

No woman has been able to resist me before, and I know exactly how to play the game according to what I need.

I'm a bit of a chameleon, and I always adapt to what I feel they want.

She wants me. All of me. And I intend to show her *exactly* who I really am.

CHAPTER NINETEEN

I'm cradling the phone between my neck and shoulder, waiting patiently for the hold music to be interrupted by the sound of a hello.

I know that I have to prepare myself to take her, and after sleeping for almost five days straight, I've decided to practice. Why? Practice makes perfect, according to the old adage. I don't want to disappoint her, and I don't want to give her anything less than she deserves.

It's uncomfortable for me to sit propped up against the kitchen sink, but, apparently, I had placed my telephone in the one drawer next to it that I never look in, and that's as far as the line will go. I don't have a cordless phone because phones are useless to me, so I make do with what I have.

"Kalispell Evergreen Urgent Care, this is Abigail speaking," a bright voice finally greets me.

"Hello, yes. Abigail? This is Guy Burress," I say, my voice slightly cracking. I clear my throat in annoyance and try again. "I was there a few days ago for some burns?"

"Oh, yes," she finally says after a few moments of silence. "How are you?"

"I'm not doing too well actually," I lie. "Is there any way you can come to my home? I'm in too much pain to walk or drive as it is, and I really think I need some medical attention."

"Why not just call an ambulance?" she suggests.

Good question.

"I would rather have someone who's familiar with what's happening to re-examine me," I reply, thinking quickly.

"I'm really not supposed to," she replies hesitantly.

"Much like you weren't supposed to write me a prescription?" I say evenly. "I've checked Abigail. Even with the doctor not being at the facility, you weren't supposed to do it. I had a hell of a time getting that medication filled and I think you owe it to me to come over. We wouldn't want that little indiscretion to reach the medical board, now would we?"

I don't take pride in issuing idle threats, but sometimes they're warranted. I'm not a blackmailer by any means, I just know when to use simple words to get what I want.

And it works.

"I'll be over by seven," she relents quietly, as if coming to my home was so bad. As if she were better than coming to *me* when I've already gone to her so many times.

"I'll be waiting," I say before I disconnect the call.

I know this seems like I'm being overbearing, but you have to understand that I want nothing more than perfection for the one that deserves it the most.

I also know that today is the day that I must spill blood in my home. With as much as I detest the thought of it, it's what needs to be done. And for just this once, I'll allow it to happen.

I know that somewhere, in one of these locked rooms, there's a cage. Large enough for a person to fit in, but it's collapsible because I needed to be able to fit it into a smaller space until it was time to use it.

Now is that time.

Or it will be at seven o'clock when Abigail arrives.

I walk through my home opening and closing the doors trying to remember where I put the fucking thing when it dawns on me. Turning on my heel, I walk back toward the living room and pull open the closet door.

There it is.

Brand new and unused.

I had hoped to use it for *her,* but I don't have time anymore. In just three hours, Abigail will arrive, and we will begin our descent into an abyss filled with pain, acts of depravity, and a desperation for life that one never feels until they're at the whims of my pleasure.

Verona felt that in her final moments, as did Laura, and that's all I've had to savor until now. *Salve. Don't forget the salve.*

"Yes, thank you."

I stop what I'm doing for a moment and wonder if I honestly answered myself out loud, before I shrug and pull the cage to a standing position. It's quite easy to assemble as it's already done; just a few firm tugs here and there, one hard shake to make sure it's standing, and it's ready for use.

I don't know who'll go into it first, but I do know that we'll both have a moment inside. Abigail's time inside of it will be longer than mine, and that's the price she'll pay for being in my company.

She'll learn to enjoy it for as long as I deem to keep her in the cage. She'll see that it's a special thing that I'm doing for her and she'll be so happy that she came. The unfortunate thing? I can't let her leave; she knows my name, where I live and, if she's smart enough, she'll most likely tell someone where she's going, but time will tell.

I guess it's time for a few confessions.

Montana isn't my actual home; I followed my prize here.

I've been to almost every state trying to find her since that one time I ran into her in the biggest city I had ever been in.

My cabinet comes with me wherever I travel because it's a trophy case really.

I might stay here when it's all said and done. As I've said, I enjoy watching the night sky over the void; the horizon is quite beautiful when you stop to actually look at it. Dusk or dawn.

There's a knock on my door now, and it's too soon for Abigail to be here. It's my delivery, and I have to take them around the back of the house to bring in my items so that they don't see my metal structure of perilous pleasure.

I won't be long.

CHAPTER TWENTY

Perfect timing.

The delivery crew is leaving now after some small talk. The two men were quite impressed that I was able to move all of those items by myself throughout the store. I gave them some tips on how I keep myself in the shape that I'm in.

I kept them there after the delivery because I just felt the need for some company I could talk to and not kill.

They were very kind.

John and Raymond they're called, and they've been doing their job for five and ten years, respectively. Before they leave, they tell me that if I need help with my "project" that they would be glad to return at no cost and assist me.

I assure them I can handle it just fine and shake their hands when they leave. The smile on my face is due to Abigail arriving. I see her driving up the driveway as John and Raymond are leaving and motion to her where she can park.

Has it already been three hours? It's possible; as I've said, I have no need to know time frames. I'm just assuming that she's arrived at the appointed time.

She gets out of her car—a small burgundy thing with a hatchback—and waits behind her still open door.

"Glad you could come," I greet her warmly.

She nods but stays behind her door. I know what she's doing; I'm not a fool. If she perceives me as a threat, it would take nothing but a few swift movements to get back into the safety of her vehicle.

So, I'll charm her.

"It's nice to see you again, Abigail," I say, stopping short of the front of the car and digging my hands into my pockets. "I apologize for how I behaved earlier on the phone, I just really wanted to see you again."

I can see her muscles relaxing, and her jaw isn't quite as tight as it was when she first stepped out of her car.

I decide to go in for the proverbial kill.

"I just couldn't stop thinking about you. I know it may seem inappropriate, but the thought of possibly having your hands on me again has moved something inside of me that I can't quite place. I hope this isn't too forward, or a hazy dream of a man that's yearning for that touch again, but I just had to let you know."

Her eyes; they tell me that I've won her over. I do much better with words than I do with touch because I can control what I say. I can lather my words in a sultry, low tone and pretty much hypnotize whomever I speak to. My touch is not quite as controlled, but I'm sure you've gathered that.

"Doing some home repairs?" she asks, crossing her arms loosely over her chest. The basic human instinct to survive is starting to show in her standoffish pose and I smile kindly.

"I will be soon enough. It's nice to have the supplies on hand ahead of time," I reply with a chuckle.

Her eyes lower to the ground for a moment. She's wondering if she should stay, and I understand, however, she's come this far, and I won't let her leave just yet.

"Would you like to come inside?" I ask brightly. "We can have a glass of wine and talk."

I don't wait for her answer; I turn away from her and begin to walk toward the back of my home. My movements are similar to subliminal advertising in when we see something grandiose, without realizing it, our minds decide we want it, and the rest falls into place.

My smile widens when I hear her car door close, followed by the sound of her setting the alarm via her car remote, then the quick shuffle of her footsteps as she attempts to catch up to me.

I won't leave her behind, but I don't tell her that as I turn the corner of my home and wait patiently by the back door. I force my eyes to fill with a kindness I could never feel as I open the door and step back, letting her walk in.

"Ladies first," I say in the most gentlemanly tone I can muster.

She steals a glance at me as she walks by, but her steps are no longer hesitant. She's confident in the fact that I most likely want her here for sex.

But sex is never the point. It's purely coincidental, if and when it happens, and I feel nothing each and every time. She's here for a greater purpose. I follow her into the kitchen and silently crack my neck.

"Red or white wine?" I ask her.

It's merely a distraction.

I won't pour wine for someone who's so easily ensnared in a net of simple words. I wait patiently for her to set her bag down on the kitchen counter and when she turns to look at me, I'm a mere few feet away from her.

Watching her.

Silent eyes telling her what's to come.

And as she opens her mouth to reply, I step forward and grab her around the throat pressing down tightly until she goes limp in my arms.

CHAPTER TWENTY-ONE

I don't like to crouch for long periods of time, but I can't help watching her. She's been out for quite some time now, and hopefully she'll be regaining consciousness soon.

It's a beautiful thing to see. She's in a fetal position, still in her blue scrubs, and her mouth is slightly open. Her breathing is somewhat ragged, and I reach through the small square holes in the cage, gripping the inside of it tightly, wondering how much pleasure I can derive from her.

How long will she last?

"Abigail," I say softly. "It's time to wake up now."

She moans slightly at the sound of her name and her legs give a lazy kick, but her eyes are still closed.

"Abigail," I repeat a little louder this time. "It's time to play."

She gasps and pushes herself up to a seated position so quickly that I almost lose my footing. It takes a lot to startle me, but that seems to have done the trick.

"Where am I?" she asks frantically.

Her eyes, the way her body is reacting, it reminds me of how one feels when they have a dream that they're falling.

Quick, sudden, terrifying; a lot like what I would imagine the last time felt like for me. Of course, I haven't slept well in years, so I can't really recall.

I get to my feet and look down at her. There are tears in her eyes now, but I assume it's due to her body jerking her awake rather than out of fear.

"I'll give you a moment," I say as I walk out of the living room.

I can only hope she doesn't scream. I can't take it when they scream; it hurts my head, but you know that already.

I walk into my room and lie down on the floor in front of my bed. There's a large wooden trunk underneath it that I was saving for a special occasion—*the* special occasion—but I want to make sure I get this right. My hand grips firmly around the wrought iron handle, and I drag it out from beneath the bed.

I clear my throat as I lean down and grab both handles, then stand, and carry it back to where Abigail is patiently waiting for me. There's a loud clanging sound. Almost as if something is slamming against metal, and when I enter the room I find the source of the noise.

It's Abigail, furiously punching at

the walls of the cage trying to get it to buckle under her frantic movements, to no avail.

"It's no use, really. I've had that specially made, and while I had hoped to use it for another, I've decided that I need to practice. So, I must say that I appreciate that you came over so willingly. Whether you live or die is up to you; I usually take into consideration what others want from me and you'll be no different. At least, not in that aspect," I say as I set the trunk down on the carpet.

"Let me out of here!" she screams at me.

I roll my eyes and undo the latch that sits right of the middle. I hate that it's not directly where it should be, but I won't let that consume me right now.

"I'm going to have to ask you not to raise your voice, Abigail. It gives me a terrible headache if I have to endure the sound for too long, and I tend to lose a grip on what I'm doing. I wouldn't want to hurt you in the wrong ways," I say quietly as I pull back the long, black cloth that sits neatly on top of the treasures inside.

A soft sigh escapes from somewhere within me. Something reminiscent of a child's innocent joy at being gifted a trove of wondrous toys.

There are a number of things in here that I can't mention just yet but know that I'm elated at the delicacy of items before me.

The first thing I remove is an iron collar. It's held in place in the back with a bolt, and I know it's meant for me by the sheer size of it.

Abigail let's out another scream, and I wince slightly. I stand back to my full height and pull my shirt off, giving her a deadly glare, before I secure the collar around my neck. It's strong, thick, and weighted; the coolness of the metal makes the hair on my arms stand up.

She watches as I reach back and push the bolt into place, eyes widening with frightened madness, and I can feel myself losing the will to stay a man. To stay the one thing that will separate me from a mindless killer, and I embrace it.

It's like a free-fall into the unknown, and each time is a precious gift because I never know if I'll return.

I roll my head as much as the collar will allow, and then glance back down into the box. I see what I want to play with, what I know I'll never use on *her,* and crouch down to retrieve it.

It, too, is heavy, made of wrought iron, and worth every penny I spent on this box. It cost me a great sum of money, but the pleasure I'll derive from it will reimburse me in the accolades I'll achieve with its contents.

"I just need one more thing," I say to her in a soft, shallow voice not quite my own.

I walk toward the door that leads to my underground freezer. I move quickly because I don't want her to lose herself in the hysteria that has descended upon her. I want her to be able to enjoy what I do to her, even if her pleasure is built from pain.

I pull the door open to the freezing room and quickly glance around, until my eyes fall onto what it is that I need. It's still bloody, but I don't care.

It'll get bloodier still, and then I'll dispose of it when the time comes. Or maybe I'll keep it as a souvenir and lay it on the bottom shelf of my precious cabinet.

Only time will tell.

I walk out of the freezing room and run up the stairs back to my home. I may have closed the door, but I'm not sure. It doesn't matter really, because the low temperatures will be there when I need them to be.

Now, with my bloodied shears in one hand and a heavy fireplace poker in the other, I'm ready to begin.

CHAPTER TWENTY-TWO

I'm not proud of myself.

Not for how I begin our game. I poke at her through the small, square holes in the cage trying to make contact with her, but she continues to press herself against the wall of the structure furthest away from me.

I scoff and finally pull open the door to let myself in. I keep my body aimed toward her as I reach back and close it, locking it securely and almost dropping the set of items I'm now trying to balance in one hand.

"Are you going to fight me, Abigail? For your life?" I ask quietly as I shift the shears back to my left hand.

"You had better kill me if that's your intent, otherwise I'll fucking kill *you*," she yells at me.

I smile.

I've never been threatened that way before. In all of the years I've been doing this, not once has anyone threatened to take my life if I failed to take theirs. I really didn't have any intentions to end her, at least not this way, but the fight in her tells me that I'll have no choice.

"And who knows that you're here?" I ask as I slowly start to circle her. She moves to the center of the cage, ready for a fight. I'm so impressed with her. I appreciate her will to live, and I wonder if her resolve will prove to me that she's worth setting free.

"Everyone! I told everyone in the office where I was going after work! They're going to come looking for me!" she hollers loudly.

I let out a sigh and drop my head for a moment. Then I look back up at her and smile.

"Thank you."

"Didn't you hear me, you fucking freak? You're going to get caught this time!"

"You're lying. Would you like to know how I know? Because if you had told anyone that you were coming to my home, you would have said nothing. You would have denied the fact instead of spitting out a childish lie. This isn't the first time I've done this, as I'm sure you can tell, and it won't be the last. I have one more after you then the world will be allowed to proceed without me. But first ...."

I move quickly, but she does too. I swing the poker as violently as I can toward her, and I miss. She moves out of the way in the nick of time, and I almost lose my balance.

Focus.

I turn to face her. I won't miss this

time. I just have to wait for the opportune moment to strike.

And it presents itself when she runs toward me. I quickly raise and bring down the poker on the side of her head knocking her to the ground. She's whimpering now; crying like a wounded animal, and it makes me feel godly for the smallest of moments.

I like to stand above my prey; to assert that I am the dominant one, and that they should be humbled to stand, kneel, bleed, beg, or cry before me.

I have no more words to offer Abigail. I have nothing left that would be a comfort to her, so I don't waste my breath. Instead, I simply get to work.

Dropping the poker to the side, I take the shears in both hands, raise them high above my head, and bring them down with full force.

She gurgles, coughs up a small amount of blood, and her body writhes. She'll go into shock soon and then she'll be as okay as she can be impaled on my living room floor.

I sit down to her right and slide the poker into her hand then turn my back to her. I close my eyes and wait patiently before she starts to strike me like I thought she would.

And just like that, the pain is back. The moments I thought I had lost to Verona are back again as the poker scratches down my back. She's not strong enough to lift it right now, but the scratches, they're drawing blood, and that's more than enough for me. I need this pain, I deserve it, and I sure as fuck have earned it.

"Harder, please," I say quietly.

I can hear her behind me, still gurgling, trying to hit me with the poker instead of raking it down my back, but it's to no avail, and I take a small amount of pity on her.

Pity amuses me.

It's not something I feel often, but I reason it's because she's *her* friend, so I turn to face her and remove the poker from her hand.

"Thank you for everything you've done for me," I say to her, tilting my head to the right. "Would you like it to be over now?"

She turns her face away and coughs, another spurt of blood covering her face. She won't answer me, but she doesn't have to. I know she wants the pain to stop, and I know that I'm the one that holds that power now.

The only question is how will I do it? Since she won't answer me, I only see one way.

"Last chance, Abigail. Would you like it to be over now?" I ask her softly, crouching over her body.

She turns her face toward me, slowly, shaking, and spits blood onto my face. I close my eyes so that I can wipe the blood away then I open them to look at her again.

Like a wounded animal, her eyes are still trying to intimidate me. Her face, while contorted in pain, is wearing a mask of fear.

I place my hands on the top of the shears, gripping them firmly, when she finally speaks.

"Why are you doing this to me?" she asks in gasping breaths.

"Because you were foolish enough to say yes," I reply simply.

She lets out a guttural sound as I pull on the shears; down, raggedly, all the way until I hit her pelvic bone. That's the only thing that stops me. While her eyes are wide and her breaths are becoming more shallow, I reach down and begin to pull her stomach open, each side to its place. I feel something odd when the warm blood touches my hands. I know what I need to do in order to consider this a successful experiment. I know what should happen, to know that I am genuinely ready for her.

She's still alive, but barely, as I pull my pants off. My cock is hard and ready as I carefully pull my boxers off around it. I have to do this quickly because I find it boorish to fuck the dead.

I crouch over her and very carefully lower my cock into the gaping flesh that's covered with blood, and I fuck her. I fuck her until I can feel her insides move, until I slip in between her intestines, and the slithering feeling reminds me of the neck that I had curiously inserted myself into so long ago.

It's warm, wet, and welcoming, and I can't help myself. I drop my knees to either side of her body and continue fucking her until I see the light go out of her eyes. Until I realize that I'm losing myself too far in the moment, until I grit my teeth and cum deep inside of her.

It was more the sound of the blood, the warmth of it, that helped me get off as quickly as I did rather than the act itself.

I'm breathing heavily as I lower myself gently on top of her. I managed to finish just before she died, and I'm pleased with myself. It tells me that I'm much more controlled than I think I am, but now it's time for me to clean up. I have to erase every trace that she was ever in my home, and I have to clean my shears. They definitely have earned their place in the cabinet.

CHAPTER TWENTY-THREE

It took three days of cleaning and careful tidying to eradicate the memory of Abigail from my home, but it's done now.

I've slept for as many days and am feeling like a different man; a more confident man. I know that I will find her today. I've done enough research going through Abigail's phone to have been able to locate *her* address.

In my snooping, I've learned that the blue Chevy Impala was actually a rental car because *her* car was in the shop. I've learned that it's much easier to get rid of a small, burgundy car with a hatchback than I've realized, and I've learned that she knows about me.

Funny the things we find out once we actually sit down long enough to understand the circumstances of what's around us every day.

I'm walking out of my home now. The concrete bags and the bricks have been lain by the appropriate windows and the doors that will house them when I'm done.

When it's finally over.

I close the door behind me as I fish for the very last cigarette of the half pack I've had for days and light it. I'm a bit nervous because I don't know how she'll receive me or if she'll even recall my face, but I am determined.

As it turns out, she never really lived very far from where I've set up my home. She's been very close this entire time, and it vexes me slightly that I never really knew this.

I'm usually very good on the

details, but since I can never recall what she looks like, I've never been able to place her long enough in my mind to know her if I've seen her casually.

I only ever see her when I'm not thinking about her, which is far and few in between. On those rare moments, when I allow other things to consume my thoughts, is when I see her. It's a bit of a conundrum, but I've handled it just fine until now.

Her home is less than a mile from mine, and I've decided to walk today. I don't want to approach her in a vehicle, mostly because I don't remember where the hell I put mine, but also because I think a nice walk back to my home will give me time to remember her fondly and to have a nice conversation.

Something small to stimulate my mind before she overtakes my senses again.

I don't know how I'll entice her back to my home, but something will come to me quickly enough to gain her trust. Maybe she's smarter than Abigail, maybe my charm won't work on her, but I'll find out shortly.

I pull on the cigarette a bit harder than I would have liked to and cough slightly. I'll never get used to having the hollow smoke of death making its way down my throat and into my lungs. It's a good thing that I'm not a smoker.

I come to the first crosswalk and wait patiently, nervously, for the blinking hand across the street to turn into a walking person so that I may proceed.

I wonder if she thinks about me in a bad light? I wonder if she knows everything there is to know about me or if she's already drawn conclusions?

I hope it's neither, because what she knows of me so far isn't truly who I am. It's what she's being led to believe. I can and will change her mind about me.

The sign changes and I walk

quickly to the other side trying to remember what street to turn on. All of them are a blur to me, most likely from the excitement of what's to happen.

But I'm good with numbers and I've remembered the street names as such so that I can continue on, knowing that my mind would be clouded with thoughts of giddiness.

On the next street, I'm supposed to turn right, then two blocks over I turn left, and her house will be there. I wonder what it looks like, I wonder if she's happy there, and I wonder if she'll miss it when she's with me. She won't suffer for long, I refuse to allow that. I just want her head; it's the only thing that'll make me feel whole again. I haven't procured her crown yet, but I've ordered it, and it should arrive in a few days.

I'll keep her alive long enough to see it; she deserves that much.

How many blocks have I walked lost in my thoughts of her? One?

Two? I'm not sure, so I turn around and glance up at the street name above me.

My heart is beginning to race. I'm on her street now and I've moved much faster than I thought I would. Her house should be in the middle of the street somewhere ... Ah, there it is.

My mind feels like the walls are caving in as I walk toward it. It's nice; quaint and small enough for one person, yet I assume the inside could house a family.

Things aren't always what they seem, are they? I try not to judge things by how they appear on the outside.

Oh, God.

I'm standing at the end of her walkway and I have to find it within myself to move my feet forward. I feel like stone has been built around them and I don't know if she's home. I don't know if she's waiting for me like I hope she is, but I have to try.

I close my eyes for a moment, take

a deep breath, and flick the cigarette before I open them again with renewed purpose.

I see a small window with the shade partially open. No one will think anything of it if I peek inside. I don't look like a prowler, and the myth is that they usually strike at nighttime anyway.

I make my way toward the side of the house as quickly as I can before I lose my nerve and use the shade of the trees to mask myself from any neighbors that might be watching.

I don't know what I'll say if one of them asks me what I'm doing, but chances are they're all at work or out for the day anyway. Mindless errands, being slaves at their day jobs; it didn't matter to me as long as they didn't interfere.

I take a deep breath as I slowly lean into the window and glance around inside. At first, I don't see anything enticing. There's a table, a sofa, a large flat-screen television, and a lounge chair. I feel the air leave my lungs in deflated defeat when the chair slowly starts to swivel.

A leg drops down, and my breath catches in my chest. She's reading my story, I can tell by the way she looks at the device she's holding, by the way her eyes are opening.

Our eyes meet, and I smile.

I ... I guess you know by now, don't you?

You'll open the door when I knock. You have to. We've come so far already.

Don't you understand?

Don't you see?

It was you.

It.

Was.

Always.

You.

FREE BOOK

Grab your FREE copy of What Lies Beneath by scanning here:

"The atmosphere is dark and ominous, and there's seemingly no escape from the monster. But the question is, who is the real monster?" – USA Today Bestselling Author Ellie Midwood

ABOUT YOLANDA OLSON

Yolanda Olson is a USA Today Bestselling and award-winning author. Born and raised in Bridgeport, CT where she currently resides, she usually spends her time watching her favorite channel, Investigation Discovery. Occasionally, she takes a break to write books and test the limits of her mind. Also an avid horror movie fan, she likes to incorporate dark elements into the majority of her books.

View Yolanda's books by scanning here;

Printed in Great Britain
by Amazon